THE LAST ROSE

Also in the Sisters Ever After series

→ SISTERS EVER AFTER ←

~THE~
LAST ROSE

Leah Cypess

DELACORTE PRESS

Text copyright © 2023 by Leah Cypess
Jacket art copyright © 2023 by Maxine Vee

All rights reserved. Published in the United States by Delacorte Press, an imprint of Random House Children's Books, a division of Penguin Random House LLC, New York.

Delacorte Press is a registered trademark and the colophon is a trademark of Penguin Random House LLC.

Visit us on the Web! rhcbooks.com

Educators and librarians, for a variety of teaching tools, visit us at RHTeachersLibrarians.com

Library of Congress Cataloging-in-Publication Data
Names: Cypess, Leah, author.
Title: The last rose / Leah Cypess.
Other titles: Beauty and the beast. English.
Description: First edition. | New York : Delacorte Press, [2023] | Series: Sisters ever after ; book 4 | Audience: Ages 8–12 years. | Summary: "The fourth book in the Sisters Ever After series of fairy tale retellings, this is the wild story of Mera, the only one who can save her beautiful older sister when she is kidnapped by the Beast who viciously rules over their small village"— Provided by publisher.
Identifiers: LCCN 2022039195 (print) | LCCN 2022039196 (ebook) | ISBN 978-0-593-48133-2 (hardcover) | ISBN 978-0-593-48134-9 (library binding) | ISBN 978-0-593-48135-6 (ebook)
Subjects: CYAC: Sisters—Fiction. | Characters in literature—Fiction. | LCGFT: Novels.
Classification: LCC PZ7.C9972 Las 2023 (print) | LCC PZ7.C9972 (ebook) | DDC [Fic]—dc23

The text of this book is set in 12.5-point Golden Cockerel ITC Std.
Interior design by Megan Shortt

Printed in the United States of America
10 9 8 7 6 5 4 3 2 1
First Edition

To my in-laws,
Dr. Sandra Cypess and Dr. Raymond Cypess—
literary analysts, dog interpreters, and
loving and supportive grandparents

⫸ PROLOGUE ⫷

My earliest memory is of huddling with my sister in front of our house, watching the castle where the Beast lived.

Usually, we didn't say anything. We just looked at the castle, with its uneven towers and crumbling battlements. We had a soft blue blanket our grandmother had crocheted, wide enough to cover us both, and we would pull it up to our chins and press against each other for warmth.

Sometimes Darina told me stories about our mother. Sometimes we talked about what it would be like to live without fear. Often we fell asleep and woke at dawn, cranky and aching and cold.

On some nights, though, we heard the hounds howling in the woods. Then we gathered our things and hurried indoors. We shut the door and wedged a chair against it. Our grandmother would let us sleep in her bed, and our dreams would be haunted by the sounds of the Wild Hunt searching for prey.

I knew, even then, that we wouldn't be safe from the Beast forever. A part of me was always waiting for him to come.

But I never thought that when he did, it would be for my sister.

Darina was not the town beauty back then. She was just ordinarily pretty, with wild flyaway hair and gangly, noodle-like limbs. Which still made her miles prettier than me. My features looked like they had been stuck on carelessly by someone in a bit of a rush, while she looked like she had been carefully sketched by a master painter.

By the time she was eighteen and I was eleven, my looks hadn't changed much, but she had grown fully into hers. Which was why, when she disappeared into the castle, nobody else in the village was surprised. She drew everyone's eyes, every day. Of course she would draw the Beast's attention, too.

I was the only one who knew that something had gone terribly wrong.

I didn't tell anyone the truth. My guilt was a boulder stuck in my chest, and talking about it would have made it worse. Besides, no one—except maybe

Grandma—would have believed me. I could imagine the scornful eyes and jeering laughs that would have followed if I'd spoken out loud what I knew to be true.

That Darina had been kidnapped by mistake.

That the one the Beast should have taken was me.

Y ou'd think that when your sister gets kidnapped by the evil Beast who has terrorized your village for centuries, people would leave you alone. Give you some space. Respect your grief.

You'd think that, if you hadn't met the people in my village.

The morning started with Foren the woodcutter pounding on the front door. When I finally stumbled downstairs, still dressed in my nightclothes, he explained that he wanted to know if he should reduce our winter order of firewood "now that you and your grandmother ... er ... won't be needing as much ..."

"As much warmth?" Grandma said crisply, having finally made it downstairs. She was also in her nightclothes, but somehow, *she* managed to look dignified. (It helped that her nightgown was made of white silk and lace and fell elegantly to her ankles, while mine was one of Darina's old tunics that came down to just below my knees and was always falling off my shoulder.) "It's my old bones that need the warmth, Foren, and our house hasn't gotten any smaller."

The truth was, the house *did* feel like it had gotten smaller in the few months since Darina had been taken. Smaller and darker and lonelier, without Darina there to dance as she set the table or to laugh at Grandma's sharp tongue. I didn't say so, though. I stomped upstairs to get dressed and let Grandma deal with Foren.

But she wasn't there to deal with my sister's most devoted admirer, Sederic, who accosted me when I was on my way to market that afternoon and brooded lengthily about how heartbroken he was. Or with the fruit-seller, who gave me an extra apple "to help with what you're going through." (How was an apple supposed to help? Especially since it was a yellow apple, blech.) Or the fishmonger, who leaned over the counter of his stall and said, "We all still miss her. But that's the trouble with beauty, isn't it? You can't be sure whose attention it will attract."

I left without buying any fish. Which meant we'd have vegetable pottage for dinner that night. Grandma wouldn't be happy, but then again, what *could* make her happy these days?

It had been three months, two weeks, and four days

since either of us had been happy. I could remember, in precise detail, the last moment when life had been good. I had woken up in bed with sunlight on my face, already excited because it was the day of the village soccer game. I'd yawned and stretched, then turned to start the torturous task of getting Darina to wake up.

And found myself staring at an empty bed.

With anyone else, I might have thought she'd gotten up early. But this was Darina. She'd once slept through someone dumping a pitcher of ice water on her head. (In my defense, she had promised to wake up early that day to build a snowman with me.) And her boots were gone.

My gut had twisted with a sick, clenching dread, even before I glanced out the window toward the outhouse and saw no sign of her.

I vaguely remembered screaming for Grandma, and leaping onto the floor, and getting my legs tangled in my blanket, and falling flat on my face. I'd had a bruise on the side of my forehead for days. Grandma hadn't mentioned it—perhaps she hadn't even noticed it—and Darina, of course, hadn't been there to badger me about it.

We knew at once what had happened to her. Everyone knew. We had all been afraid of it our entire lives.

Since then, every morning, I kept my eyes closed for

an extra half second before I woke. I opened my eyes and turned, and Darina's empty bed hit me like a blow.

After storming away from the fishmonger's shop, I couldn't face the town square, where most of the other village children were playing. None of them had ever had much to say to me, except when their parents forced them to; now that everyone knew what had happened to Darina, all they had were nosy questions and pitying looks. So instead of going home that way, I crossed to the other side of the market and started down the forest path that bypassed the village. It would take longer, but unlike everyone else in the village, I liked being in the woods. And I was in no rush to get home, especially now that I'd finally managed to be alone. . . .

"Mera! There you are! Wait for meeee!"

My shoulder blades tightened. I considered picking up my pace. But I knew there was no point.

Darina's friend Ressa fell into step beside me. That would have been enough to ruin what was left of my day, but when I glanced over my shoulder, her younger sister Talya was trudging reluctantly behind her. Talya met my eyes and gave me a look that made it clear she was no happier about this encounter than I was.

Ressa and Darina had been friends—*were* friends—and

Talya and I were supposed to be friends because we were the same age and our sisters were friends. This was an expectation that both of us found burdensome.

Sure enough, as soon as Talya caught up to her sister, she said, "Can't I go back? I was in the middle of a game of marbles. And I was winning."

"Hush," Ressa said. "You can play with your other friends later. Mera needs you now."

"I really don't," I said, without much hope that Ressa would listen. Usually, Ressa avoided the woods even more zealously than the rest of the villagers, since she favored silly shoes that made walking on rough ground treacherous. She had clearly followed me on purpose. Which meant there was no chance of getting away from her.

"I saw you talking to Sederic earlier." Ressa looked demure, with her long black hair always wound into neat braids, but she had a knack for being the first to know every bit of gossip in the village. Darina called it a talent. I had another word for it. "He looks like he hasn't slept in days. Did he tell you how he's feeling?"

He had. At length. But the subject of Sederic's pining for my sister could go on forever, and I was not in the mood. I shrugged.

"I heard he wrote a new song about Darina." Talya's

voice, as usual, had a sharp edge that could make even the most innocent comment sound like an insult. "Do you know if that's true?"

He had written several songs. Sederic was in training to be a minstrel. Since there was no one in our village to actually train him, what that mostly meant was that he spent his time writing verses, singing them, and modestly accepting the villagers' compliments about how talented he was.

His voice *was* excellent. His verse-writing skills, though, could have used some constructive criticism. And also, a little more variety in their subject matter. I loved my sister more than anyone, but there were only so many songs you could hear about her before they started getting repetitive.

"I heard he was going to try to rescue her," Ressa said, sighing. "He swore that he would release her from the Beast's clutches, even if he died in the attempt."

Talya rolled her eyes—for once, not at me. Nobody in our village's history had ever escaped the Beast's castle.

"Well," Ressa amended, "he wrote a song about his determination to rescue her, and what would happen when he tried."

"What would happen?" I asked, before I could think better of it.

Ressa's eyes shone. "He would die horribly with her name upon his lips."

"And would she be rescued?"

"No." Ressa clasped her hands together over her heart. "She would never know of his sacrifice. With his dying breath, he would call her name, and she would hear it from her dark, dank prison cell beneath the castle—"

"Never mind," I said.

"No one can *rescue* her," Talya snapped. "The Beast has surely turned her into one of his hounds by now."

I bit my lip on a protest. Everyone in the village knew that was what the Beast did to the people he took: he turned them into hounds and forced them into his pack, to run with him on the Wild Hunt and terrify the people who had once been their friends and neighbors.

"It's just a song," Ressa said. "The castle doesn't even have a basement. So the cell wouldn't be *beneath* it. She was held in one of the towers." She bit her lower lip. "Probably."

We all turned and looked at the Beast's castle, with its high, jagged tower on the north side and its stubby round tower rising from the south walls. It looked deceptively close, even though it actually took hours to reach it by foot. Its silhouette was so familiar that staring at it felt unnecessary. But like everyone else in the village, I stole glances at it anyhow, constantly. How could I not?

For as long as anyone could remember, the lord in the castle had been an inhuman, monstrous creature, hated and feared. A Beast who led his pack of hounds on the Wild Hunt, to chase down and kill anything that caught their fancy. Not just wild animals, but people's cattle, and pets, and sometimes the people themselves.

We all knew how to stay safe from the Hunt. We kept out of the woods at night, and we retreated into our homes at the first sign of howling. It was easier to avoid than storms or flood or fire.

But sometimes the Beast came alone, stealthy and unseen, and we only knew about it when someone disappeared. Not killed, but stolen. Not ripped apart, but *changed*.

The Beast took only one or two people every generation, but everyone had an ancestor or distant relative who had been stolen by the Beast and turned into one of his hounds, bound to his will and to the Hunt.

Ressa prattled on, but I stopped paying attention. She was saying something about time and courage and hope; it was as if she'd taken a bunch of inspirational words and shaken them carelessly together. Talya, meanwhile, was giving me her usual contemptuous look, like she wasn't sure how I dared breathe the same air as her.

An ache rose in my chest, so thick and heavy that I couldn't breathe. I didn't want to be here with them. I wanted to go home and complain to Darina, then roll my eyes when she told me that I should really try harder to be friends with Talya. I wanted to return to a home that had my sister in it and be annoyed because she was taking too long with the hairbrush or wearing impractical clothes. Most of all, I wanted the life I was now living to not be my life. I wanted that so badly it hurt.

But Darina wouldn't be home. Only Grandma would be there, sweeping up the kitchen and grinding her herbs and, soon, making a fuss about the lack of fish. Going through the motions of life, just like I was, and pretending it was bearable.

I knew of only one way to escape the feelings slamming together inside me. I thrust my basket at Ressa.

"I forgot to get fish," I said. "Would you take my basket to my grandmother, please? She needs the eggs immediately."

"Oh, of course!" Ressa said, oozing kindness.

"Actually—" Talya began, but Ressa gave her a sharp look and she fell silent. She shot me a glare as Ressa pulled her down the path.

I rolled my eyes. If Ressa thought she was going to extract gossip from my grandmother, she was a fool.

Then again, she *was* a fool. So that was probably exactly what she was hoping for.

Not that I was one to talk about foolishness. Not given what I was planning to do.

I looked again at the castle and clenched my fists. Everyone else might have given up on Darina, but I had not. I never would. I was just waiting for my chance.

And when it came, I was going to go to that castle and get my sister out.

2

I hadn't told anyone about my plan to save Darina. Not even Grandma—*especially* not Grandma. I knew what they would all say, which meant I didn't need to hear it.

So instead of wasting my strength on fruitless arguing, I reserved my energy for spying on the castle. I had snuck away a dozen times since my sister disappeared, prowling the area around the castle and watching for any hint that the Beast was getting ready to lead his hounds on the Wild Hunt.

When he did, Darina would be in the castle alone. Unguarded. At least, I hoped so.

The Beast has surely turned her into one of his hounds by now.

Talya had a way of making statements so confidently that all denials sounded pathetic. But that didn't mean she was actually right. After all, I knew things that Talya did not. It was impossible to imagine Darina—sweet, gentle Darina, who coaxed spiders out of the house instead of smashing them—running with the Hunt.

My sister was still human. She had never been anything but human. I knew it deep in my bones.

I tore my eyes from the castle and glanced in the other direction, to make sure Talya and Ressa were out of sight. Then I turned off the wide path onto one of the many narrow trails that led deeper into the forest.

The trail was well trodden and littered with crushed leaves. After a few yards, I turned again and made my way straight through the underbrush, pushing between low-hanging limbs and hopping over a muddy, trickling stream. Branches cracked under my feet and thorns caught at my skirt. I ducked under a fallen tree, straightened, and walked right into a dangling spiderweb. I brushed its sticky film off my face, spat into the mud, and decided that I had gone far enough. I could see nothing around me but mostly bare branches.

It wasn't wise to be so deep in the woods on my own. It was, to be precise, forbidden. My mother's body had been found in the woods, back when I was just a baby, and Grandma had always told us to stay away from the forest.

But I had been cautious for so long, and it felt like fighting my own self. I wanted to be reckless. I wanted to be wild. I wanted to be the thing that *was* feared, not the thing that was afraid.

The problem with you, Darina had said to me once, *is that you can* know *something is stupid and do it anyhow. It would be less frustrating if you were just plain stupid.*

She had been referring to my attempt to string a clothesline from our window to the oak tree behind our house so we could zip down it as a faster way of getting outdoors. And *that,* for the record, had been a phenomenal idea, and would definitely have worked if Grandma hadn't stopped me. But Darina wasn't wrong. Sometimes I *liked* doing things that I knew were unlikely to end well. To free myself, just for a moment, of the constant thinking and planning and worrying that ruled every second of Grandma's and Darina's lives.

For the past few months, with Darina gone, Grandma had been too worried about her to hover over me. That had been even worse, because I'd been forced to do all the caretaking and planning for myself, to keep from causing Grandma more grief.

I was so tired of it. And everything about today made me want to throw it off, to set loose the wildness inside me. To believe that I could get Darina back.

I took off the pouch that hung around my neck. It was weighty and solid in my hand, packed full with the rose powder that Grandma had given me when I was only a toddler.

Her voice whispered in my memory: *Be careful, Mera. Don't attract the Beast's attention.*

But we'd already caught his attention. The worst had happened. What was left to be afraid of?

I hid the pouch under some crackling leaves. Then I straightened. A fierce, powerful rush surged from deep within me. I closed my eyes and drew in a breath. The pull welled up within me and spread, my skin tingling so sharply it almost hurt—

The branches behind me rustled.

My eyes snapped open. I whirled.

A white hound stood beside a broad-trunked tree, its eyes focused on me. It was completely still, stiff-legged and alert.

In a hunting animal, complete stillness is never a good sign.

I stared back, my heart pounding. The hounds normally hunted only in their pack, led by the Beast. I had never before seen one alone. I had also never seen one this close. It was a solid, majestic figure, slightly larger than a wolf. Its narrow, triangular eyes were amber, and its sleek, thick fur was pristine white. Everything about it spoke of pure, coiled power.

Why was it here? Did it know, somehow, what I intended to do? Had the Beast sent it to scout out any would-be rescuers and kill them?

Don't be ridiculous, I told myself. How could the Beast know what I—or anyone—was planning? But there was something about the way this hound was staring at me. Like it recognized me, and was furious, specifically, at *me*.

I didn't know what to do—keep looking at it? Run? No one had ever told me how to act if I came across one of the Beast's hounds. Probably because it wouldn't make a difference. If one of them came after you, you were dead.

But this one wasn't coming after me. Yet. It was just... looking at me.

"Hey," I said in a soft, shaky voice.

The hound drew its teeth back. Its ears flattened against the side of its head, and a low, rumbling growl rose from its chest.

Oops.

The hound opened its mouth so wide that its muzzle seemed larger than its head, its yellowed teeth glistening and wet. It drew itself in, ready to leap, and I closed my eyes.

There was a whoosh of air—and then nothing.

Several silent seconds passed. I managed to open my

eyes. The forest was empty, the nearby branches rustling slightly. There was no hound there at all.

It was another few moments before I could move, since every part of me was still convinced I was about to die. It took me longer to force myself to walk, on quivering legs, back toward the village. I jumped every time a twig cracked or a leaf rustled.

And it took even longer to realize I had forgotten my pouch, retrace my steps, retrieve it, and go back up the trail toward the village again.

By then, I was finally convinced that no hound was going to leap from the underbrush and kill me, but I wasn't so certain I was safe from my grandmother. The sun was setting in a golden glaze against the darkening woods, and I should have been home long before to help her prepare dinner. Now that Darina was gone, Grandma relied on me to gather the firewood and lift the heavy kettle and take over the dicing when her wrist started to ache.

And now that Darina was gone, she worried about granddaughters who weren't home when they were supposed to be.

I hurried along the path as fast as I could, heading back toward the village instead of taking the longer way through the woods. By the time I reached the town square, the sun had set and the shops were closed. The only person I saw was Sederic, who was wandering the streets looking melancholy. When he spotted me, he veered in my direction. "Mera! Have you heard—"

"No," I said, and dashed past him.

He watched me go with a mournful expression, and guilt pricked at me. Sederic's dramatics weren't pretense. They were his way of trying to let people know what he genuinely, truly felt. Darina had always tried to be kind to him and had given me sharp looks when I made fun of him.

But Darina wasn't here to be disappointed in me.

I turned onto my street. Our home, at the end of a steep slope, was a fine, sturdy wooden structure, far too big for two people. The lights in the kitchen were on—I could see that from here—filling the windows with a warm, flickering glow.

As soon as I saw the house, I realized the true reason I was so late. I didn't want to go home. In the village or the woods, a tiny part of my mind could pretend that things were normal. It had always been my job to go to the market in the afternoon, and I often did it by myself. Nor was this the first time I'd snuck off into the woods. But once I was home, sitting across from Grandma at the large round kitchen table, just the two of us . . .

So what? I demanded of myself. *Is it better for Grandma to eat alone?* Shame drove me swiftly up the street to face my grandmother's anger, which I fully deserved.

But I needn't have felt guilty. She wasn't alone.

When I opened the door to the kitchen, there were two people sitting at the round table. One was my grandmother, her face pinched and sharp, her eyes focused on the other—a man with his back to me, so all I could see of him was his ragged blue cloak and the small round bald spot in his grizzled hair.

I knew who he was even before he turned around. His face was drawn and lined, as if he had aged a decade in the year since I'd last seen him, but it was still familiar.

"Hello, Mera," he said.

I closed the door behind me. My chest felt tight. I didn't know why *he* was here, but I was sure of one thing: he was only going to make everything worse.

"Hello, Father," I said.

3

My father blinked at me as if he had forgotten who I was. Behind him, Grandma's face was completely blank.

"I came," my father began, then cleared his throat and started again. His voice was gravelly and halting. "I came from the castle."

"The *Beast*'s castle?" I exclaimed. As if there were dozens of castles scattered around our village to choose from.

My father and my grandmother both ignored that question, as it deserved. I chose a better one. "Why were you in the castle? Did you—" A sudden leap of hope. Maybe I was wrong. Maybe he *was* here to help. "Did you go to rescue Darina?"

"No," my father said. He leaned forward, bringing his face closer to the lamp's light, and I saw that his cheeks were streaked with trails of dried tears. "She came to rescue me."

I couldn't even come up with an adequate question. I just stared at him.

"The Beast kidnapped me first." His throat convulsed. "That's what caused all this. Darina found out that he was holding me prisoner, and she came to trade herself for me."

"I don't understand." I glanced at my grandmother.

"Don't look at *me*," she said. Her eyes were sharp and glittery, despite the huge purplish hollows beneath them. "I'm hearing this for the first time, too. I just got home."

Got home from searching for me, presumably. But I didn't have any space left inside me for guilt. Not over anything I had done *today*, anyhow.

My father took a deep breath. "Four months ago, I came here—to the village—after my last trading expedition. But I didn't tell anyone I had arrived. Instead, I went straight to the Beast's castle."

"Why?" I said.

"I had heard there was a magical rose in the castle, one that could perform wonders, and I thought . . . I wanted it." He looked down. "It would be extremely valuable, and my fortunes have taken a bad turn lately. That rose could have saved me—saved all of us—from poverty."

I glanced at my grandmother. She had told me about the Beast's rose.

But her attention was trained on my father. "Are you really that stupid?" she demanded. "Did you think the Beast wouldn't catch you?"

His shoulders rose and fell. "I was desperate. I wasn't thinking straight."

My eyes narrowed. My father was a lot of things, but he wasn't stupid or impetuous. He liked to fill pages with charts and plans before he did anything. There was something he wasn't telling us.

"The Beast did catch me," my father admitted.

"How unexpected," my grandmother said.

"I didn't really believe the tales about him, but—he's as monstrous as they say he is." My father shuddered. "I thought he would kill me. Instead, he threw me into a cell. He demanded that I send a message to my daughter and tell her to come trade herself for me."

My mouth dropped open. "And you *did*?"

"No! I refused. But the Beast must have sent a message on his own. Because after a week—" He drew in a shuddering breath. "She came. She agreed to stay in the castle in my place."

"An excellent bargain," my grandmother said. "Very advantageous for you. I can see why your trading ventures have always done so well."

I should perhaps mention at this point that my grand-mother is my *mother*'s mother. And she and my father had never gotten along that well.

My father managed to meet Grandma's gaze for a few seconds. Then he sank against the back of his chair. "I tried to talk her out of it. You must believe me. For months, I refused to leave without her."

"And yet," my grandmother said, "it seems you left eventually. Because here you are."

"I had no choice. I wasn't doing any good there." He swung his head around and looked, not at my grand-mother, but at me. "If I could have saved her by staying, I would have. You must know that."

"I don't know that," I said. "I don't know anything about you."

He flinched, and something sharp lodged in my throat. I wasn't trying to hurt him; I was just telling the truth. My father had left, as often and for as long as he could, ever since my mother died. Even when he visited the village, he spent more of his time at the tavern than he did with us. Grandma had raised me and Darina. We trusted and loved *her*. My father was a distant stranger.

A distant stranger I was constantly, bitterly angry at.

Despite that . . . I believed him. Darina had always been such a devoted daughter, forgiving my father for every absence and (annoyingly) insisting that I forgive him, too. Plus, she had that ridiculous self-sacrificing streak—I knew it well, having used it many times to get her to do my chores or let me sleep late. She was far too nice for her own good. If the Beast had asked her to trade her freedom for our father's . . .

Darina *would* do it. Of course she would.

My palms hurt. I looked down and realized that I was digging into them with my fingernails. I opened my hands quickly, but they were just fingernails, not sharp enough to draw blood.

"So she's still human?" I asked.

My father blinked again. "What do you mean? Of course she is."

It struck me, all over again, how like a stranger my father was. Not just to me, but to our entire village. There were things we all understood but never spoke of, things you couldn't learn by sitting at the tavern with other foreigners or trading with shopkeepers. Things the people who lived here grew up knowing.

Things my father, apparently, didn't know.

Grandma sighed and laced her fingers together on the table. "You know," she said to my father, "what the Wild Hunt is."

"Of course. The wolf pack that the Beast leads. But—"

"They're not wolves," Grandma said, "though they're closer to wolves than to dogs, I suppose. They are the

Beast's hounds." She had told me and Darina this story only once, many years ago; back then, her hair had been auburn instead of white, and her voice had been less tired. "Centuries ago, when the borders between worlds were more open than they are today, the Faerie Queen used to come into the human world to hunt. She rode an eight-legged horse and was accompanied by her hounds, who were bred to be single-minded and vicious in their pursuit of prey."

"What was their prey?" my father asked.

Which was exactly the question I had asked when Grandma first told me about our village's history.

"Whatever ran from them. They were not . . . discriminating. When the borders between our world and the Faerie Realms began closing, the queen decided to leave her pack in the human world, to hunt humans and remind them that she was to be feared. She appointed her favorite hound to be the head of the pack, transforming him into a fearsome Beast." Grandma put both her hands on the table. They trembled slightly; that, too, had not been the case last time she told this story. "And we have, indeed, lived in fear of him ever since. The people of this village have mostly avoided being his prey—we know enough to stay indoors when the pack runs. But we can't stop him from using us to replenish his pack by turning villagers into hounds." She stopped there and gave me a sharp look. I realized that I was leaning forward expectantly, and I straightened and tried to assume a neutral expression.

Apparently, she was not going to tell my father the rest of this story.

"Are you sure this is all true?" Father asked. "Maybe it's just a pack of wolves that has grown bold because no one will challenge them. Their howls sound exactly like wolf howls."

Grandma gave him a long, withering stare. When he did not wither, she turned to me. "Mera. Did you know that Darina went to the castle on purpose?"

"No!" I said. "How would I have known?"

"Doesn't she tell you everything?"

"I thought so." I hugged my arms to my chest. "I guess not."

Grandma's eyes softened. "She probably didn't have time. Or perhaps she thought you were too young to . . . I mean, I'm sure she was trying to protect you." She started to get to her feet, then staggered and gripped the arm of her chair. My father started toward her to catch her, but she glared at him fiercely and managed to lower herself back down on her own.

I bit my lip. My grandmother was so stern and

competent that I forgot sometimes—most of the time—that she was actually quite old. Too old to be raising two girls by herself. Too old to be dealing with any of this.

"Well," my father said, "regardless, Darina is *not* a hound. She was human when I left." His fingers traced quick, random circles on the surface of the table. The few times I had seen my father baffled by a problem, he had covered pages and pages with scribbles while trying to work it out.

(My grandmother, I could safely guess, had not offered him paper or pen.)

He noticed what he was doing and pressed his hand flat on the wooden table. "If this tale about hounds and Hunts is true, it only means it's more urgent that we get her out."

I opened my mouth to respond, but Grandma shot me a warning look, and I shut it. Grandma shook her head slightly, her message clear: *He can't handle it.*

I didn't really care what my father could handle. But looking at my grandmother's weary eyes, it occurred to me that, actually, it was Grandma who couldn't handle any more of this. She wanted my father gone, and I could hardly blame her.

"Maybe we should talk about this tomorrow," I said.

"No," my father protested. "You don't understand—"

I laughed. I didn't plan to, but I couldn't help it. "We're

the ones who live here. We understand all too well. None of *us* would have been foolish enough to go into the Beast's castle to begin with!"

My grandmother clicked her tongue against her teeth, but didn't say anything. My father ran a hand over his hair and looked at me helplessly.

That felt familiar. My father didn't know me any better than I knew him. Even when he stayed with us, he liked talking to Darina a lot more than he liked talking to me. She was sweet and forgiving, and never sulked or glared at him or harped on how long it had been since he'd last bothered to show his face.

Almost every conversation I had with my father ended with him looking frustrated and helpless, and then giving up. Which was no surprise. My stubbornness made lots of people give up on me.

He had focused, instead, on Darina. He'd had such high hopes for her. When he did visit, he had devoted himself to her future: teaching her table manners and the proper way to speak, trying to get her music lessons (unfortunately, the only music teacher available was Sederic), showing the village seamstress the latest fashions from the cities. He always said her "accomplishments" (by which he meant her beauty) would secure her a bright future in a big city, far from our isolated, provincial village.

"I think," Grandma said faintly, "that it might be best if we all went to bed."

My father's jaw clenched, but after a moment, his shoulders sagged. "Very well. I can rent a room at the inn for the night." He got to his feet. "I'd better go quickly. When I left the castle, it seemed like the Beast was preparing to hunt tonight."

I startled, then tried to hide it by brushing my hair away from my face. Since there wasn't any hair *in* my face, it probably wasn't very convincing. Luckily, neither my father nor my grandmother was looking in my direction.

It didn't occur to me until the door swung shut behind my father that he had probably been hoping we would offer him a bed in our house.

Once he was gone, the silence settled on the kitchen, thick and smothering but also comfortingly familiar. There was no need for either me or Grandma to say anything. We ate swiftly and sparsely, and then Grandma went to bed, gripping the rail tightly as she made her way carefully up the stairs.

I cleaned up, and then I sat alone at the table, staring at its familiar scratches and stains. There was a dark blotch from the time when Darina and I had tried to dye some cloth purple, and a deep gouge from an incident involving a carving knife and some unripe pumpkins.

It seemed like the Beast was preparing to hunt tonight. If my father was right, it meant my chance had finally come.

I waited until I heard Grandma's breathing grow deep and even (which is the polite way of saying I waited until her snores shook the house; Grandma sounds like a bear when she sleeps). Then I got up and let myself out of the house.

I stood for a moment right outside the front door, watching wispy clouds brush against the moon. I wondered if Darina, too, had hesitated before going to the castle to save our father. Had she stood right in this spot? Had she thought about turning around and going back inside?

I took a deep breath of sharp, cold air. Then I turned down the street and started walking in the direction of the Beast's castle.

4

The village was quiet and deserted, but I kept to the shadows anyhow. I focused on keeping my feet moving, one after the other.

I thought of Darina making this exact trek, alone in the darkness. I understood now why she hadn't told anyone where she was going. It was hard enough fighting off your own fear without also having to deal with other people's reactions. She wouldn't have wanted to burden Grandma, and she probably hadn't thought there was anything *I* could do. I was just her younger sister, the one she had always tried to protect.

My turn, I thought. It sounded fierce and determined in my head, and almost made up for the fear shooting through my feet and up my legs like a thousand quivery pins.

I turned and slipped through the space between the baker's shop and the candlemaker's home, and then into the woods behind them. The ground here sloped suddenly and precipitously toward a ravine, and the thick branches of the trees blocked most of the moon's light. I kept going, the trees and their shadowy foliage closing in around me.

To most people in the village, the woods was a terrifying tangle of darkness and danger, to be avoided whenever possible. The trees here were ancient and intertwined—some had been growing since the time of the fae, and still retained a watchful aura, as if humans were upstart interlopers to be repelled. Most importantly, the woods was home to the Wild Hunt, and anything in it was their fair prey. Everyone I knew ventured among the trees only in daylight, and reluctantly even then. (Darina only went when I begged her to.) No one wanted to enter it at night.

Except me. And I had come this way often enough to make my way swiftly in the dark.

Nobody knew that—not even Darina, and certainly not Grandma. I figured that many of the villagers, especially the other children, sensed that there was something wild in me, something they didn't entirely understand. It made them uncomfortable around me, but they invented other reasons for their discomfort. My unkempt, tangled hair. My ill-fitting, unfashionable clothes. My coarse features and thick eyebrows and crooked teeth. They taunted me for those things without ever understanding the true reason they disliked me.

That's what I told myself whenever the mockery hurt. It helped. Sometimes. A little.

I didn't hesitate or slow down until I reached the creek at the bottom of the ravine, which shimmered in the moonlight like a stretch of black marble. It was fuller than usual because of the heavy rain two nights back, and some of the rocks I used as stepping stones to get across looked wet and slippery. It would have been easier on all fours, but I didn't want to pause, even for a second. I got a running start, and sprang.

The key was not to hesitate. If you tried to balance too long on any one rock, you lost your momentum. I had always been better at this than Darina, even though we had only done it during the day. She had splashed into the creek too many times to count.

I landed with a thud on the muddy pebbles on the other side and laughed out loud. Out of habit, I started to look back, as if Darina might be waiting her turn. Then I caught myself, bit my lower lip, and started up the side of the ravine.

Once I did that, there were no more memories of Darina to contend with. She had never been willing to get closer to the castle than the creek. I grabbed the occasional stunted tree or rock outcropping to help pull myself up, and didn't slow down until I reached the edge of the woods.

Then I stepped out of the trees into the weed-covered clearing that surrounded the castle. It loomed against the night sky, its grim facade dark and forbidding.

The fear came again, turning my whole body into a series of discordant quivers. The castle walls stretched above me. They were made of old, craggy stones, with arched windows set at irregular intervals. I craned my head back to look at the windows. They were large, with wide, flat sills, and as far as I could see, there were no oiled cloths or screens covering them. And that craggy wall was full of handholds and footholds....

Maybe sneaking in didn't have to involve the front door.

I approached the castle, then reached up and grabbed one stone where it jutted out slightly from the wall. I wedged my foot into a crack between two other stones and pulled myself upward.

Don't look down, I warned myself. I kept my eyes on the wall and the stones. There, another crack. And another foothold. I pulled myself up, then up again. I dug my fingers against the stone and heard a scratching sound as claws—not fingertips—scraped the rough rock.

"Mera! Stop!"

I shrieked. My foot slipped, and I clenched the rugged stone with all my might, pressing myself against the wall.

"Halt! I implore you, do not go farther!"

That was, unmistakably, Sederic. I looked down. And discovered that after all that effort, I had barely ascended a few feet.

Sederic looked up at me. His hair was slicked against his face, and water dripped from his chin—*he*, clearly, had not managed the creek crossing successfully. His clothes were caked with dirt. Sederic was the kind of person who normally changed his shirt if he got so much as a juice stain on it. The fact that he was standing there covered in mud was even stranger than the fact that he was here at all.

"Why are you here?" I hissed.

"I followed you from the village," he said.

"Why?"

"Because I know what you're doing."

I rolled my eyes. "I think it's pretty obvious what I'm doing."

"I am going to assist you."

My arms ached with the strain of holding onto the wall. "No. You're not. Go away."

"I can't let you go into the Beast's castle by yourself," he said. "You're just a child."

"So what? This would be just as hopeless if I was an adult."

He raised his eyebrows. Apparently, that wasn't an impressive argument. "I want to help, Mera."

At times like these, I could see why Ressa turned into such a fool around Sederic. It wasn't just that he was good-looking. It was that sweetness in him, that sincerity, that made you want him to be happy. To be the one who made him happy.

"I appreciate it," I said. "Really. But you need to leave. I know what I'm doing."

"I cannot stand by while the woman I love is trapped with that monster." He threw his head back. It was a move that usually made his hair fly back dramatically, but since most of his hair was stuck wetly to his skin, it just made a squelching sound. "Move aside, Mera. I'm coming up to join you."

"Does it look to you like I can move aside?" I wasn't actually sure how much longer I could hold on. "And you can't make this climb. You need small feet—"

He was already pulling himself up. He didn't even make it as far as I had before he lost his grip, slid down the side of the wall, and landed with a high-pitched yell in a patch of brambles.

So much for sneaking in.

I let go of the wall and leapt down. My feet hit the

uneven ground hard, and I pitched forward onto my hands and knees. Pain shot up my arms, but I ignored it as I got to my feet. "Are you all right?"

"No," Sederic said, sprawled awkwardly against the castle wall. "My heart will never heal."

"What about your body?"

"I cannot feel merely physical pain."

"So you're fine, then."

Sederic sighed heavily, several times. I ignored him, and finally he got to his feet. He wiped the wetness from his eyes, somehow managing to leave a single slow tear behind. "Don't give up, Mera. I will help you rescue Darina with the strength of my—"

I never got to find out what Sederic thought his strength was (though if I had to guess: eternal devotion and/or musical ability). Because at that moment, a series of growls sounded from behind him.

The darkness beneath the trees erupted into fur and teeth as a pack of hounds poured out of the forest and bore down on us.

Sederic screamed and threw himself back at the wall. I whirled next to him, both of us pressed against the stones, and braced for teeth ripping into me.

But the hounds slowed. They advanced deliberately, eyes gleaming and tongues hanging out.

Because why would you rush when you had your prey trapped?

The lead hound growled. The sound dug under my skin, making my blood race. A familiar fierceness swept through me, longing and rage and desperation combined.

Sederic stepped in front of me. I could see that he was shaking as badly as I was, and his voice, too, shook as he hissed, "Mera, run!"

To my surprise, my voice didn't shake at all. "If we run, they'll chase us. They won't be able to help themselves."

"When they go for me—" His voice caught. "When they bring me down, Mera, that's when you run."

My blood raced faster, sweeping away my fear. I lifted my chin, feeling it stretch—

And then a sound came from deep in the woods. A long, thrilling howl with a triumphant edge.

The master of the Hunt calling his pack.

The hounds all went still, heads going up, ears pricking forward. The one in the lead looked over his shoulder at the rest. Then, as one, they turned and streamed into the trees. Their movements were so smooth and graceful that within seconds, I could no longer tell where they were, or even in which direction they had gone.

Not a single one looked back at us before they disappeared.

I should have felt relieved. Instead, a vast, frustrated longing swept through me. My skin felt too tight, as if my true, wild self were desperate to burst out of it.

Don't, Mera. You'll attract the Beast's attention.

The tingle swept over me, the wildness rushed through me, and I didn't resist. Vaguely, I was aware of Sederic watching me with horror, but I didn't care. I pulled the wildness of the woods in, using the howls to drive the change faster. My senses expanded, and a tension dropped away from inside me, as if I had let go of an anchor and was about to fly. My bones reformed—not hurting, exactly, but not *not* hurting, either—and then the world was sharp and clear as my humanity dropped away, leaving me savage and focused.

My paws hit the ground hard. The howls rose from ahead of me, louder now, and—to my hound's ears—full of meaning. Behind me, Sederic screamed.

I lifted my muzzle to the sky and howled back, my breath streaming visibly upward. Then my muscles bunched and loosened as I flew across the ground, head down, tail low, rushing into the dark woods to join the rest of the pack.

5

Here was the part of the Beast's story that my grandmother didn't tell my father. She had told it to me only once, after the first time she saw me shift.

When the queen commanded her pack to hunt in the human world, she left them a gift: a flower from the Realms that, when eaten, gave them the power to shift into human form. So that they might better survive in the world that humans were making over to their liking.

It was an unwise decision. The queen did not understand the temptations of humanity, and so she did not foresee the consequences of her gift. Over the next hundred years, her hounds spent more and more of their time as humans, and eventually, they were human. The Beast was left alone, to roam the forest without a pack, feared and avoided by those who had once followed him.

But neither hounds nor humans are meant to live alone. It wore on the Beast, the loneliness and the betrayal and the endless, unfulfilled urge to lead the Hunt. It turned to bitter, consuming

anger, and then to a desperate need to turn things back to the way
they should have been.

So he kept an eye on the descendants of his hounds, and when
he saw any who were still able to shift—he took them. He lured
them into his pack and back into their true forms, and kept them
with him until they forgot how to shift into humans. Or forgot to
want to. For more than a hundred years, he has been rebuilding
his pack, reclaiming his hounds from humanity.

And that's why you must control it, Mera. You must fight the
temptation. Because if you shift, you'll attract the Beast's atten-
tion. He will know you are his, and he will come for you.

The trees flew by me, the woods full of sounds and
scents, a whole world of information that had been in-
visible to my human senses. I put my head down and ran,
with the total, effortless focus that was an essential part
of being a hound.

Then I caught up to the pack, and all at once, my focus
wasn't just mine anymore. It was shared, part of a unified
force, and the power of it swept through me.

I had only ever shifted when I was completely alone,
at times when I was sure the Hunt wasn't out in the
woods. I'd tried to shift as infrequently as I could—my
grandmother's warning was always in my mind—but

when the temptation got too great, I was at least careful. Every time, I pushed it off as long as I was able to, and I shifted back to human as soon as I could bear it. I made sure I wasn't seen. I'd told myself that I was being safe.

I'd known all along that it wasn't true. But I hadn't cared. When the temptation came over me, it was too strong.

And now Darina was paying for my carelessness. The Beast must have seen me in hound form and realized that someone in our family could become one of his hounds. He'd thought it was Darina . . . but he'd been wrong.

I was the one he'd been after all along. He must have suspected that, once he'd realized Darina couldn't shift. And now he would know it for sure.

Those thoughts had been tormenting me for weeks. But now they didn't seem to matter. All that mattered was the world around me and the chase ahead of me and the wild joy surging through me.

A few of the hounds tilted their ears at me. I was the only pup among them, but I was old enough to keep up, and I proved it as we streamed through the forest. The air was alive, the darkness no hindrance at all. We were single-minded and intent, with no need for hesitation or thought, following our master without question. To my hound's eyes, the Beast didn't look grotesque at all. He was majestic and ferocious and powerful—and I, like the rest of the pack, was ready to follow wherever he led.

He glanced back once when we got close to our prey. I tensed, but he wasn't focusing on me; he was checking on all of us, making sure we were ready, letting us know he had spotted our prey. The human part of me faltered, thinking: *Sederic?* But a moment later we all caught the scent: a deer, a little too old and a little too slow.

The Beast jerked his head sideways, and half the pack separated from the rest to create an ambush. The deer smelled us and bolted, and the Hunt began in earnest.

I had hunted before in hound form. Rabbits, mice, chipmunks. As a human, I found all those animals cute, and would try to patch one up if I found it injured in the woods. But the world looked different when you were a hound.

We raced after our prey with a grim, thrilling eagerness. It wasn't just that the ferocity didn't bother me, that the deer's terror didn't stir pity in me. There was no *me*. I was part of the pack, one with it in purpose, paws digging into the ground, head low. If I had been in human form, I would have been laughing as I ran.

Dirt spurted from beneath our paws, and the breeze of our passing swept our fur flat. The night air sparkled, cold and crisp. We caught up to the deer as it crossed the creek, and the Beast flew at it first, raking its hind-quarters with one of his massive claws. The deer kept going, running full-tilt up the side of the incline, and we plunged through the cold shallow water after it.

The other half of our pack came around, and the deer slid and scrambled, turning to run sideways. A hound flew from the underbrush and grabbed the deer's hind legs, for one triumphant moment, before a powerful kick sent him flying. But by then we had it surrounded.

We circled and feinted and bit, wary of the stag's hooves and antlers; the result was predetermined for the pack as a whole, but any single one of us could still be injured. One hound got struck in the side and had to drag himself away from the fight, and another narrowly missed a fatal stab from the deer's antlers.

I found myself, shamefully, hanging back. I was too small, and I had been too recently human. I was afraid of the fight, and a tiny, distant part of me was sickened by the deer's futile struggle—even as a larger, wolfish part of me enjoyed it.

None of the others seemed to mind my absence, or even to notice it. And when the battle was finally over, when a mass of hounds latched on to the deer and pulled it down to the ground, no one made a move to stop me as I crept forward to join them at the kill.

Then I stopped. Something deep in me, something weak and human, balked.

I had eaten raw, bloodied meat before, when I was in hound form—small animals with crunchy bones. My human self had also eaten deer meat, broiled and cut into neat slices, steaming on Grandma's plates. There was no reason this should be different.

Yet I found myself hesitating, several feet from where the others were gnawing eagerly away. The Beast was at their head, of course, eating the choicest part of the meat. As I stepped back, he lifted his head and looked at me. His muzzle was coated with black—to human eyes, I was pretty sure, it would have looked red—and his eyes glowed in the moonlight. He was huge and terrible, and vaguely I remembered that I hadn't wanted him to see me. But I wasn't afraid of him. I was part of his pack. I *wanted* to be part of his pack.

Darina, the human part of me whispered.

I crept backward, belly low to the ground. The Beast watched me, his ears pricked forward. But he didn't make a move to stop me, not even when I turned suddenly and crashed through the brush in a dead run.

6

When I emerged from the trees in front of the castle, my sides were heaving and my breath was harsh and loud. I did not give myself time to rest. I veered around the dark stone walls and skidded to a stop in front of the castle's front door. The breeze ruffled the fur on the back of my neck as I looked up.

The front door of the Beast's castle was higher and wider than any door I had ever walked through. I didn't know if that was typical for castles, or if this particular door was Beast-sized. It was made of dark polished wood, with a metal knocker in its center shaped like a wolf's head.

Pulling at the knocker might open the door. But it was far above my head. There was no way I could reach it as a hound.

I fixed the image of my human self in my mind and pulled myself back into it.

Nothing happened.

My body remained furry, my paws remained planted on the ground, and the world around me didn't spring into all the colors a human could see. I turned in a circle, growling at nothing. I hadn't had time to take off my pouch of rose powder before I shifted, the way I was supposed to, and it had disappeared into the shift along with everything else I was wearing. Grandma had given me the powder the very first time she saw me shift; she'd said it would help me change back if I ever got stuck. I'd always obeyed her instructions, though this was the first time I'd ever *been* stuck.

I licked my muzzle, then made myself go still. I gathered all my nervous energy and drew it in, but that was no good; it was a hound's energy, and it made turning human feel impossible. I tried to remember having hands, wearing clothes, reading books. I thought of Grandma, and then of Darina. I fixed the image of my sister in my mind, her large, intent eyes, her light musical laugh, the way she put one arm around me and drew me close, her hair tickling my face . . .

The familiar tingles went through me, rough and wrenching. I drew in a breath of pain and relief, and then I was crouched on my hands and knees, breathing raggedly.

I got to my feet, my legs quivering. For a moment,

standing upright felt awkward and unbalanced. I smoothed down my dress, poked my rose powder pouch to reassure myself that it was still there, and gave myself a moment to get used to my human form again. It always felt gawky and graceless after spending time as a hound.

But only a moment. The Hunt had already succeeded, which meant the pack could come home at any moment. I didn't have much time.

I was reaching for the knocker when a familiar voice said, "*Mera?*"

I whirled.

Sederic stepped out of the trees. His clothes were ripped, his hair plastered to his face, his cheeks smudged with dirt. But I didn't focus on any of that. I met his large green eyes, and stepped back from the horror in them.

"You—" It was the first time I had ever seen his eloquence desert him. "You're one of them—"

"No!" I said. "I'm not. I just—I—"

He stepped back. The expression on his face was unfamiliar, but also completely expected. Revulsion, disgust, and fear.

"I'm sorry," he said. "Mera, I'm so sorry. I should have stopped you somehow, I shouldn't have let the Beast get you—"

"He didn't!" Shame choked me. A small part of me had always been proud of what I could do . . . what I was . . .

despite how dangerous it was. Maybe because of that. But the horror and pity in Sederic's eyes made me wish I could disappear. "I'm not part of his pack. I'm going to get Darina away from him, I swear."

His eyes flickered from me to the castle and back. "But you—I saw you—"

My insides shriveled up. I hated Sederic and I hated myself. "I can't explain now. This is my only chance to get her. But please, Sederic, don't tell anyone that I'm here. Don't tell them what I—" I gritted my teeth against tears. "Don't tell them what I am."

Somewhere in the woods, a hound howled. Sederic jumped.

"Go," I said. "Quickly. And please, don't tell—"

I didn't get a chance to repeat my plea. He was gone, crashing through the underbrush so loudly that any animal within leagues could have heard him, racing with all his strength away from me.

I stood fighting back tears. He *would* tell everyone. Of course he would. By tomorrow morning it would be a song, and they would all know what I was. Grandma had known for a long time, of course, but now she would know that I had ignored her warnings, had changed into one of the Beast's creatures behind her back. I couldn't even imagine what Talya would say. Actually, I could. . . .

But I wouldn't. I didn't have time for that. I didn't have time for any of this.

I turned toward the castle, reached for the knocker, and pulled.

The door didn't budge.

I tried putting both palms against the door and pushing with all my might. Still nothing. I stepped back, frowning. My eyes went again to the knocker. The wooden wolf's head on it was watching me with narrowed eyes.

A chill went through me. I stepped sideways. The eyes didn't move—of course they didn't, they were made of wood—but somehow, they followed me all the same.

I had to be imagining it.

I wasn't imagining it, though.

My body trembled with the desire to run. *Darina*, I reminded myself. I glared back at the knocker and said, in the bravest voice I could manage (which, as it turned out, was not very brave), "Let me in."

The door swung inward, ponderous and silent.

I heard a squeaking sound and realized it wasn't coming from the door hinges. It was coming from me. I pressed my lips together.

Through the open doorway, I could make out an empty hall, nearly as dark as the night outside. I stepped closer, keeping one eye on the wolf's-head knocker. It appeared to have gone to sleep.

"Darina?" I called, then wished I hadn't. My voice was thin and wavery, and the darkness swallowed it up.

I glanced again at the knocker, then walked through the doorway. The darkness flickered, then came alight. Dozens of candles' flames flared up at the exact same time. They were set into sconces and candelabras, lining the vast, empty hall I had stepped into.

I dug my nails into my palms until they hurt. "Darina?" I whispered.

Silence.

The hall was huge, its stone floor bare of rugs or furniture. Directly across from me, a wide spiral staircase led up to a balcony. The balcony wrapped all around the walls, and an ornate ironwork railing ran alongside it. The candlelight didn't reach behind the railing. Anyone could have been up there, unseen, watching me.

I took a deep breath, then let it out with all my strength. "DARINA!"

Somewhere, a hound barked, and several others answered. The cacophony echoed around the walls. Dark, shadowy forms moved behind the balcony railings, too low to the ground to be human.

The Hunt couldn't have come back *already*. Not

without my seeing them. Some hounds must have been left behind to guard the castle.

To repel intruders like me.

"DARINA! WHERE ARE YOU?"

The barks died down, and so did the echoes of my shout. Silence settled over the hall, dark and thick.

Fear crept up my legs in a series of sharp quivers. I fought it back with everything I had, but mostly with my anger. We had all been afraid for so long, and because of that, we had let the Beast get away with everything he did to us. *I* had been afraid, for weeks, to come to this castle for my sister. Fear was the Beast's most powerful weapon, but it lived in my own mind. I didn't have to let it stay there. I could beat it back.

Or at least I could ignore it.

Or at least I could *pretend* to ignore it.

I forced my legs to move, first one, then the other, propelling me up the stairs. Behind me, I heard a low growl coming from the knocker, and my shoulders tightened. But I didn't look back. I gripped the banister tightly to make sure my legs would hold me up, and I kept moving.

At the top of the stairs, shadows stirred, revealing flickers of yellow eyes. It was darker up here, but still not pitch-black; there were golden sconces set in the walls between rows of doorways, and the candle in every third or fourth sconce was lit. The balcony ran all along the wall, and there were at least twenty doors, all shut.

A large, furry shape slid out of the shadows.

I screamed and jumped back. My heel slipped on the marble floor and went out from under me, and I fell with a thump on the top stair. I reached out blindly, grabbed the banister, and only just managed to stop myself from tumbling all the way down the stairs and breaking my neck.

By the time I pulled myself to my feet, I could see that the shape was one of the hounds, large and wolfish, with yellow eyes and pure black fur. It growled but remained where it was, lashing its tail.

Cautiously, I stepped away from the stairs, not breathing until my back was to the balcony. The hound watched me but didn't move, and I drew in a deeper breath. In human form, I couldn't sense all the ways hounds had of communicating, but I could read this one's body language enough to know it wasn't planning to attack me.

What I didn't know was what it *was* planning to do.

The hound looked at me. There was something about it . . . something familiar . . . I knelt, searching its eyes for a hint of the human it had once been. But there was nothing.

It whined softly. Then it turned, padded down the

hall, and stopped in front of one of the doors. It looked at me over its shoulder, its ears flickering back and forth.

Was it . . . *helping* me?

I didn't see how that was possible. I had only been part of the pack for an hour, and during that hour I had been completely in thrall to the Beast. Surely, none of the hounds had held on to any semblance of their humanity over years of hunting down prey with him.

I crossed the space between us and put one hand on the door. The hound gave me a sharp, encouraging bark, then turned and padded farther down the balcony, turning its head watchfully from side to side. Within seconds, it had disappeared into the darkness.

"Thank you," I whispered, hoping that was the appropriate phrase. Then I rapped on the door.

The sound echoed sharply. But when the knock faded away, silence settled in the castle again.

I flexed my aching knuckles, then tried the door handle. The door swung easily inward, and I stepped into a large, lushly decorated bedroom. A bed took up the center, with multiple layers of gauzy, lacy canopies. The walls were lined with furniture—clothes chests, a table, a mirror, and a washbasin—all illuminated by the moonlight flowing in through the large rectangular windows.

I recognized those windows. I had seen them from

outside the castle, from the lakeshore on the castle's east side.

I walked farther into the room. The bed was empty, but there were clothes heaped on the chest at its foot—half-but-not-really folded, which was typical of Darina. I didn't recognize the clothes, and when I brushed them with my fingers, they were softer and silkier than anything Darina or I—or anyone in our village—had ever worn.

I went to the window. Below me, the lake was a stretch of black marble, ripples glittering with faint silver in the moonlight. The trees' bare branches stretched over the water, reflected dimly in its black depths. Farther into the forest, I could see large birds flapping raucously above the trees, near where the hounds had made their kill.

And there, on the far shore of the lake, stood a huge, furry, apelike shape. The Beast, standing at the edge of the woods, staring straight at the castle with eyes that glowed in the moonlight.

My first instinct was to duck back. But motion was more likely to attract his attention. I dug my fingernails into the windowsill and stood very still.

The shadows around the Beast stirred and thickened, revealing themselves as hounds: smaller and sleeker than him, but with the same glowing eyes and thick, bristling fur. They gathered around him, lifted their muzzles, and howled.

The high, mournful sound rose through the night air and shivered through me. I found myself opening my mouth as if to howl back, and I clamped my lips shut so hard I bit myself.

The Beast and his hounds turned abruptly and slid among the trees, like a stream of deadly, disappearing ghosts.

A flash of jealousy pierced me. I backed into the room, away from the window, from the howls I still imagined echoing in the night air. I wrapped my arms around my body.

Then I heard a low, threatening growl behind me.

I whirled. The room was silent and empty, and for a second I was sure I had imagined the growl. The image of the Beast and his hounds was so fresh in my mind. . . .

Then I heard it again, and realized: it was coming from inside this room.

More precisely: from under the bed.

It was a high bed, with thick wooden legs and lots of drapery hanging over its sides. Very fancy. Very . . . *concealing*. There was definitely enough space under there for a hound.

My heart pounded against my ribs. I looked around the room for a weapon. Everything was lace and gauze, pretty and useless. There might be something other than clothes in one of the three chests along the wall, but I would have to turn my back on the bed—and whatever was under it—in order to open them. No way. The wardrobe might have something—shoes with sharp heels, perhaps?—but I would have to walk past the bed to get to it. Also not happening.

There was nothing here that would help me. The only question was: run or fight?

Run, every inch of my body screamed. But the hounds were hunting animals. If I ran, it would chase me, and it would catch me.

I drew in my breath and bent my knees, my pouch thudding against my chest, a familiar tingle crawling up my spine. My lips drew back, and I snarled at whatever was under the bed.

It burst out in a cracking of wood.

My vision filled with a mass of fur and teeth and claws. Every emotion but one fled my mind: utter, abject terror.

I turned and ran.

7

I burst through the doorway with the hound's hot breath on my back, saliva splattering my ankle. Shut doors and flickering candles flashed past me on one side, and the wrought-iron railing flew by on the other. Behind me, the hound snarled and lunged, and teeth grazed my skin.

I let out a sob. I couldn't outrun it in human form, and if I paused to shift, it would be on me before I had a chance.

But my human form did give me one advantage: hands.

The hound gathered itself and lunged again. I threw myself sideways, straight at one of the doors, and yanked its handle down. Behind me, the hound skidded on the floor and turned to throw itself at me again. If this door was locked—

The handle gave under my hand with a click. The

door swung open, and I flung myself through into a narrow hallway, then whirled to slam it shut.

Too late. The hound was already halfway through.

I spun and kept running, glad that this door had led into a hallway rather than a room. The hallway was lined with thin arched windows, the moonlight turning the floor into patterns of darkness divided by lines of musky dimness. It was so narrow that my hands kept hitting the stone walls as I ran, but the pain barely registered. Something crackled beneath my foot, but there wasn't enough light for me to see what it was. Behind me, the hound's paws hit the floor in smooth, relentless bursts, and panic gave me the strength to launch myself faster—

—straight into the flat stone wall at the other end of the hallway.

Pain shot up my arms as I crashed into the wall, breaking the impact with my forearms. I turned to one side, then the other, hoping for a bend in the passageway. But I already knew what I was going to see: stone walls surrounding me. There were no passageways branching off, no sharp turn I hadn't seen. This was a dead end.

It didn't make sense. I looked frantically for some kind of hole, or doorway, or *something*. Why would anyone build a passageway that led nowhere?

I let out a sob and slammed both palms against the

wall. A part of me hoped it would move, or break into pieces, but all I did was hurt my hands. A lot. There were two dark spots higher up on the wall, but when I reached up, they were just nails jammed between the stones. I tugged on one of them, but it didn't cause the stone wall to swing inward or anything useful like that. It just hurt my hand more.

The hound stopped, watching me with calculating, eager eyes. I could almost feel its lazy, pleasurable anticipation of the kill. I had felt it myself.

I turned my back to the wall. More crunching beneath my feet, but I didn't look down. I looked only at the hound.

"I'm not prey," I said to it, and I shifted.

The second my paws dropped to the floor, I realized what had been crunching beneath my shoes: shards of broken glass. They cut painfully into the pads of my paws. I ignored them and focused on the hound in front of me, whose stance had shifted from *hunt* to *fight*. It bared its teeth at me. I bared mine back.

For a moment we just stood there growling at each other. I knew I couldn't actually fight him, even in hound form; he was almost twice my size. But I could tell that he wasn't sure whether to attack me or not.

I wondered why he was hesitating. The fact that I was young wouldn't matter to him—wolves regularly hunted and killed newborn pups from other packs. Maybe my shifting marked me as a member of his own pack.

Several seconds passed, and the hound part of my brain took over. It wasn't interested in the reason for his hesitation. It was only focused on taking advantage of it.

I gathered my legs under me and rushed him, then dodged sideways at the last second. The passageway was so narrow that I had to squeeze between the hound and the wall; for a moment, with fur in my face and stone scraping my side, I wasn't sure I would make it through. He could have trapped me, or crushed me, just by pressing his weight sideways.

Instead, he tried to turn and bite me. He didn't have enough space, and by the time he figured that out, I was through. I raced down the hallway and through the open door, back onto the balcony. I hurtled full-speed alongside the railing.

I kept my eye out for a stairway, and when I found one—not the grand central staircase, but a dusty wooden back stairway—I practically threw myself down it, pummeling toward the ground floor.

It was nearly pitch-black in the stairwell. The only windows were narrow slits in the walls that barely let in any moonlight. I tripped over my front paws and fell down the last couple of stairs, landing in a sprawl on a straw-covered stone floor.

The pain pierced my panic. I scrambled to my feet and stood still, my breath loud in the silence. But that was the only sound; there were no snarls, no barks, no rush of paws. The hound had not followed me down the stairway.

Of course, I didn't know what might be waiting for me here at the bottom of it.

I spent a few moments panting and sniffing the air, until my sides stopped heaving. Then I lifted my head and looked around.

I was in a large, echoing room, with the remnants of tapestries dripping down stone walls. Moonlight flowed in through wide, arched windows that lined one wall, sparkling off a huge chandelier and illuminating a long wide table. The windows were framed by the ratty fragments of velvet drapes, and the tablecloth that hung from the table was long and embroidered with lace, but threadbare and faded. There was a chair at each end of the table, and place settings laid out in front of the chairs. In the center of the table was a platter of roasted chicken, with several loaves of bread laid out around it.

The chicken smelled moist and spicy, and my stomach grumbled. That awkward, silent dinner with Grandma had been a long time ago, and I hadn't eaten much. Obviously, I wasn't actually going to *eat* food that belonged to the Beast . . . but even as my human mind urged caution, my hound's senses were enraptured by the scent of the chicken. I couldn't stop myself from padding over.

The edge of the table was scored with long, deep marks, as if scraped by giant claws.

I stopped. Fear rushed over me again, but I fought it back. I called up an image of my sister's face, her soft, kind smile, her large, steady eyes.

I drew myself inward to shift back into a girl.

Nothing happened. This time, there wasn't even a hint of tingling; just a vast, wolfish confusion. For a moment I forgot what I was trying to do and why. The scent of roasted chicken flooded my nose, and I turned, salivating, toward the food.

Someone laughed, low and tinkling.

I whirled, tail lashing. My eyes and my nose told me there was no one else in the room. But that taunting, feminine laugh rang in my ears.

I sniffed the air again—it was, instinctively, my first way to locate anything—then pricked my ears forward. The laugh was coming from the corner, where the drapes from two windows met, providing plenty of concealment for someone to be hiding. But my nose still told me there was no one there.

Fur bristling, legs stiff, I approached the corner. I grabbed a corner of a drape with my teeth and tugged it back, every muscle braced to attack or be attacked.

But there was no one behind the drapes. There was only an unframed rectangular mirror leaning against the wall.

As I let the drape go, that laugh flickered through the room again, and it came—unmistakably—from the mirror. Something black and sharp passed behind the glass, and I felt eyes focus on me before the drapes fell over the mirror again.

Because of the drapes, the voice I heard was muffled. But it was unmistakably the same—person? creature?—that had been laughing at me. "Go, my hound. Hunt for me."

I backed away, a growl trapped in my chest. My fur felt like a thousand pins.

My hound. It sounded like a caress, and also like a command. This, I knew suddenly, was why I couldn't shift. Because something in this castle wanted me to stay a hound.

No, I thought. I glared at the drapes and whatever was behind them. *NO.*

Again, that laughter. But I couldn't tell if I was hearing it or merely remembering it.

I pulled on everything human within me. I drew on

my determination to save my sister and my anger at my father and my hatred of the Beast. A hound couldn't hate the Beast, but *I* did. He had taken my sister and destroyed my family and I *hated* him—

My skin shivered. My bones tingled, and I welcomed the sensation even as it sharpened into pain. I screamed. And heard, as if from a distance, my scream turn from animal to human.

I crouched on the floor, panting, and stared at my familiar jointed fingers.

Something hissed. I turned my head and looked at the drapes covering the mirror. One of them fluttered.

I scrambled to my feet and ran.

I circled the table with its steaming platters and pushed open the door on the other side. I had just a moment to see, by the light from the dining hall, a staircase ascending in front of me. Then I slammed the door shut and enveloped myself in darkness.

I leaned back against the door, gasping. Several moments passed in silence: no laughter, no chase, no sound at all from the room behind me. I still felt the urge to get farther away from it. I slid my foot forward until it hit a step, and then I started up the staircase, keeping one hand on the dank stone wall. This stairway was narrow and rickety, the steps shifting sideways under my feet.

But no dust rose as I walked; it might be ill-maintained, but it was well-used.

Another curve in the stairs, and the blackness turned gray. There was a light somewhere up ahead. In a way, that was more terrifying than the darkness. I forced my legs up, and up—and then, quite suddenly, I was on a landing, where a faint fall of moonlight from a high-up window turned the solid darkness into dimness and shadows. My eyes, which had been straining to see, could easily make out the barely lit space. Straight ahead, another set of rickety stairs ascended upward and curved into darkness. To my right was the door to a prison cell, set into a stone wall. The door was made of wooden bars that stretched from the floor to the ceiling. It was so wide it took up more space than the wall did.

I walked across the landing until I could see through the bars. The stone floor of the cell was bare but for a chamber pot—fortunately empty—and a metal band, clearly meant to be snapped around someone's ankle. The band was connected to the wall by a long chain.

Caught in one of the twists of the chain was a strip of bright blue fabric.

My throat went dry. I knew what I was looking at.

This was where my sister had been imprisoned by the Beast.

I gripped the wooden bars of my sister's prison cell. Their smooth polished coldness chilled my palms, and I snatched my hands away, making the door swing open.

I stepped back, and back again, until my shoulder blades pressed against the far wall. To the side of my head, an empty candelabra jutted from the stone, melted wax clinging to its sides.

Darina. How long had she been chained here, at the mercy of a monster? And where was she now?

I should have come sooner. I *knew* the Beast wanted me, I knew she was here by mistake, and I hadn't come to save her. I had told myself I was waiting for my chance, but the truth was, I hadn't come because I had been afraid.

Of course you were afraid. You're an eleven-year-old girl, and he's the Beast.

The soothing voice in my mind sounded like Darina.

Of course it did. She had always been the one reassuring me, forgiving me, doing her best to soften my rough edges—or to pretend they were soft. She had never been angry at me, not *really* angry, though I had, at times, given her plenty of reason to be. Her goodness had softened her view of me, and I'd let her believe what she wanted. I'd let myself believe it, too.

But standing alone on the landing, staring at the chain that had bound my sister, it was so clear: I should have come sooner. Much sooner.

Above me, something growled.

I tried to step back again, forgetting that there was no more *back* to step into. My head hit the stone wall so hard that my eyes watered. I blinked them clear and looked up, straight into the amber eyes of a lean gray hound glaring down at me from the top of the stairs.

Honestly. How many hounds were in this cursed castle?

As if to answer my question, another hound appeared behind the first, and then another. Three hounds snarled at me, teeth sharply white beneath their narrow, gleaming eyes.

Three of them, and this time I was truly trapped. The stairs below led straight to a closed door, and I wouldn't have time to open it. There was nowhere to run, no escape, and they were here to hunt.

I could shift.

But I remembered that taunting, triumphant laughter, and I shuddered. Something in this castle—or maybe the castle itself—*wanted* me to be a hound. If I shifted again while I was here, I wasn't at all sure I would ever be able to shift back.

Then again, if those hounds killed me, it wouldn't really matter.

I glanced at the bars of the prison cell, calculating distance and speed. The hounds slunk down the stairs, and I forced myself to move. One quick dash across the landing.

The movement roused the hounds' hunting instincts, as I had known it would. They lunged down, all three at once, huge and heavy and snarling, and I lifted the door latch, flung myself into the cell, and pulled the barred door shut behind me.

Teeth tore at my arm, ripping my sleeve and my skin. I let go of the door and stumbled farther into the cell. The fastest hound growled in frustration, shoving its lean muzzle between the bars, a saliva-drenched strip of my sleeve dropping from its jaws. The other two hung back, watching with vicious eyes.

I hoped desperately that the latch had dropped into place when I shut the door. I didn't dare get close enough to check. Blood dripped from my throbbing forearm, twining down my wrist. I could tell by the hounds' focus that they smelled it. One of them lunged, slamming its huge body against the bars. The door shuddered, and I screamed despite myself. If the latch or the hinges broke—

But they didn't break. The door held firm. The hounds dropped back, watching me.

Then the gray one padded over to the door, went up on its hind legs, and nosed the latch.

At first, I didn't understand what it was doing. Then it maneuvered one paw under the latch and nudged it again with its nose, and I got to my feet and leapt for the door, determined to hold it shut.

Another of the hounds sprang toward me, but I had no choice: without the bars between me and them, I would be dead in seconds. My only hope was to stop them from opening the door. Luckily, I had a pretty good shot at that. Even if they could figure out latches and try to open them, they only had paws and teeth, and I had human hands with fingers and thumbs. Not quite as good for fighting, but *much* better at keeping doors closed.

The hound working the latch dropped back down on its haunches, then leapt up, snapping at my fingers with its teeth. I snatched my hands out of the way, but I didn't step back from the bars.

The hound stretched up on its hind legs again, reaching for the latch. I put my hands back on the bars, and this time, the other two hounds leapt straight at me, fast and simultaneous. I felt hot, wet breath on my fingers before I pulled my hands away. The snap of teeth was so loud that I curled my fingers into my palms, flinching at the thought of those teeth crunching into my bones.

The gray hound growled and twisted its head, and I heard the latch fall against the bars. The other two hounds gathered themselves, watching the door with a terrible eagerness.

The door swung slightly outward, and they danced back to give it space. Then the gray hound pulled it open wider with its front paw.

Terror pounded through me. I knew I should grab the manacle, at least have some sort of weapon—but I was paralyzed with fear and couldn't move. The gray hound squeezed into the cell, snarling and eager, and then I couldn't think either.

"*STOP.*"

The word echoed through the stairway, and the hounds froze. They turned their heads, and the hound in my cell slunk out backward.

The Beast appeared at the top of the stairwell.

He was so big he barely fit; his huge, furry, muscled body squeezed between the walls, and he slid down the stairs as if they were a ramp, his clawed feet too large to fit on any of the narrow steps. The hounds themselves were beautiful, in a fierce, deadly way—at least, they were if you saw them from a distance—but the Beast was something else: a creature that was half hound and half man, with elongated arms and a fur-covered head and slavering jaws. His fur was mottled gray and black, and his eyes were narrow above his thick, powerful muzzle.

The hounds pressed together and backed away, watching him—not afraid, exactly, but wary. He stopped and stared at them, his eyes glowing.

"Go," he said to them, and they turned and disappeared down the stairs. His voice sounded like it was scraping over gravel, yet the strength of command in it was so overwhelming that I never doubted his hounds would obey.

I was pretty sure that if he turned that voice on me, I would obey him, too.

The Beast stopped on the landing. His face was like a wolf's head that had been half-squashed into a man's, all bristling fur and shortened snout and triangular ears that looked like horns. But his eyes were the worst. They were narrow and yellow like a hound's, but there was something *human* in them.

I wanted to pull the door shut, but I knew there was

no point. The Beast could open it if he wanted. The Beast could do as he pleased, to me or to anyone. No one could stop him. No one had ever been able to stop him.

"Where is my sister?" I demanded. My voice shook so badly that it was even less intelligible than his. But I got the words out.

Those yellow, inhuman-yet-human eyes narrowed. He sat back on his haunches, his fur bristling.

"I know why you're here," he said. His voice was like a wolf's growl forming human words. But the words were entirely understandable. "You're here to take her away from me. But you won't. She's mine now."

She was alive. A fear that I hadn't even acknowledged rushed away from me.

"She's not part of your pack," I said. "She never was." I swallowed hard. "I—I'm the one who can be one of your hounds. *I'm* the one you want."

"Not anymore." His tail lashed against the wall, raising a cloud of dust. "Go home, Mera. Leave her be."

I jumped. "How do you know my name?"

"She told me."

I gritted my teeth. "I want to see her."

The Beast's lips curled back, revealing curved white fangs. "No. You'll ruin everything." He swung his head sideways, bringing his eyes closer to mine. A bit of saliva swung off the corner of his mouth and splashed on the stone floor. I stared at his huge, fur-covered face, my breath frozen with a new surge of terror. "You shouldn't have come to my castle."

"I came for Darina. You took her by mistake." I couldn't believe I was sitting here arguing with this monstrous creature who could break me with one swipe of his paw. But he still hadn't hurt me . . . and there was something in his voice, beneath the angry growl. Something vulnerable. "She's not one of yours. Let her go."

And take me instead, was how I had intended to end that sentence. But the words stuck in my throat, and I couldn't make them come out.

The Beast snarled. "She is free to go whenever she wishes. She wants to stay here."

Yeah, sure. "Then why won't you let me see her?"

"Because you think I'm a monster!" He rose to his full height, which was nearly to the ceiling. I whimpered and fell back. "She will see me through your eyes, and she will hate me again."

And there it was, the vulnerable thing. He was *afraid*.

"She hates you *now*," I said. "She's only here because you kidnapped our father!"

"Your father is a thief," the Beast hissed. "He came here to steal my roses. I had a right to kill him. I showed him *mercy*." His eyes narrowed. "As I did to the other human man who followed you here. I let him leave the castle grounds, and held my hounds back from kill-ing him." He paused, like he was waiting for applause. When I didn't respond, he added a bit sulkily, "Darina convinced me that it was no longer appropriate for the pack to hunt humans."

So not because he objected to killing people on prin-ciple. Obviously.

"I'll let you leave, too," he said. "I'll have a hound escort you safely home."

Such a thoughtful offer. "I'm not leaving until I see my sister," I said.

The Beast's mouth curled. He reached forward and pushed the door shut, then pulled up the latch. It clicked loudly into place, locking me in.

Then he turned and loped down the staircase, leaving me alone in the cell.

9

Once you're in the castle, the Beast locks you in a cell and leaves you there to starve. Then, when you're hungry enough, he changes you into a hound.

No, he gives you food, but he never lets you out. When you go mad, that's when the change happens.

He waits until you're starving, and then he sets his hounds on you. They rip your limbs apart, and if you survive long enough, he makes you one of them.

There were a lot of stories, theories, and wild imaginings about what the Beast did to his prisoners. But they all had the same starting point: he locked them up.

I had told myself I didn't believe those stories. But apparently some part of me did, because when the latch clicked shut, I lost the ability to think. I threw myself at the bars, pounding and kicking.

"LET ME OUT! COME BACK! LET ME OUT *NOW!*"

Obviously, there was no response.

By the time logic pierced my panic, my hands hurt and my voice was raspy from screaming. I backed away from the door and looked wildly around the cell. There was nothing to see but the small window near the top of the wall, moonlight shining off its close-set bars. No escape there.

I tried to stick my arm through the door bars to reach the latch. The space was too narrow. I couldn't push past my elbow.

Finally, I checked the gash on my arm, which turned out to be little more than a scratch, though one that had produced plenty of blood. I used the chamber pot, pushed it into the corner, then knelt to examine the iron band chained to the wall. The chain was rusted, huge and heavy; if I could unfasten it, I would at least have a weapon.

Which was a ridiculous thought. It was a manacle and chain. It had literally been designed to be impossible to unfasten.

Still, I picked up the chain. It was so heavy I strained to lift it. The bit of blue cloth fluttered slightly—

Wait.

I dropped the chain with a thud that reverberated through the cell. The cloth ripped free and hung between my fingers. It was smooth and silky, and when I held it closer to the moonlight, I saw that it was the deep, brilliant blue of the lake at midday.

I remembered my father sitting at our kitchen table, his ragged blue cloak covering his shoulders.

It hadn't been my sister who was locked in this cell. It had been my father.

My mental image of Darina quailing and weeping dissolved. I opened my fingers and let the scrap of cloth flutter to the dusty floor.

If there was anything I knew about my father, it was that he was not the type to quail and weep. Maybe the Beast had broken him eventually, but until then, he would have been *thinking*. My father loved to solve problems. Even—especially—when those problems were not solvable.

I remembered him scribbling on paper, crumpling pages in his hands and throwing them away, his pencil twirling in his fingers. I knew what he would have done while locked in this cell.

I went to the wall and began moving slowly along it, my face inches from the roughly hewn stone. I found what I was looking for right under the window: tiny letters scratched into the mortar between the stones, barely legible in the moonlight. They were low on the wall—my father must have been sitting when he made them. I got down on my hands and knees and twisted my head back and forth, trying to get the best angle of moonlight on the words.

It was impossible. There were vines growing around the bars of the window, blocking much of the light. I thought I could make out some words—*Beast* (not a hard guess), *prisoner . . . find*. But nothing else.

I sat back. A wave of dizziness came over me. All at once, I realized how exhausted I was.

And I couldn't read the words until morning anyhow, so . . .

I looked around the dim, empty cell as if hoping a pillow or blanket would magically materialize. Then I turned on my side and curled up on the stone floor, resting my head in the crook of my elbow. I thought wistfully of my own warm, soft bed, where I had spent so many nights these past few months staring at the ceiling, unable to close my eyes.

But there, on the rough stone floor of the cold lonely cell, I was asleep within seconds.

———————◆———————

I woke to the sound of the cell door opening.

I leapt to my feet, instantly alert. The cell was still dark and dim; even the moonlight was gone, but now there was light coming through the bars of the cell door.

I blinked at the light for a second, which was all the time it took for the Beast to slide a bowl into the cell and slam the door shut.

Then I dove across the floor, even though I knew it was too late. My foot hit the bowl, sending thick, lumpy stew spilling everywhere. I grabbed the bars of the door and shook them—or tried to. They didn't budge.

The Beast glanced at the spilled stew. He was holding a candelabra in one hand, and its three long candles lit the landing better than the moonlight had. "There isn't any more of that."

"I don't want to eat," I snapped.

My stomach chose that moment to growl loudly.

"*Here*," I added. "I don't want to eat in this cell. Let me out."

"I don't wish to keep you captive," he said.

"Wonderful. Then don't."

Something savage flared in his eyes, and I let go of the door and stepped back. He leaned forward, putting his shaggy face up against the bars. "I thought you might be hungry. Or . . . bored. If you want, I could bring you a book."

"A *what?*"

"A book?" He looked uncertain, like he wasn't sure I knew what the word meant. "Your sister likes to read them."

I could actually imagine it. Darina, trapped and alone, distracting herself with a book instead of building up her rage.

"She likes books even better than she likes flowers." He chuckled—*fondly*—and heat flushed through me.

"Thanks so much," I snarled. "I'm not in the mood for reading right now."

"Neither was Darina," he said. "At first."

He had *no right* to say her name like that. As if her accepting books from him, when he had kidnapped and imprisoned her, was an endearing memory.

"Until when?" I said. "Until you starved her into submission and forced her to eat meals with you in that rotting dining room? How did that work, exactly? Do you even *eat* human food?"

"I can," he said. "Darina taught me to use utensils, too." He chuckled again. Like his voice, it sounded *wrong*, human sounds being forced through a shape that had never been meant to hold them.

Some of my reaction must have shown on my face, because his amused expression dropped away. "I won't let you take her away," he said. "She's happy here."

"Is she?" I knew it was stupid to argue with him. But for whatever reason, it didn't seem like he was going to kill me. "How happy do you think she'll be when she finds out that you kept her sister imprisoned and let me die of starvation?"

His tail lashed the wall behind him, so hard it knocked some rock fragments loose. "I am not starving you. I came here to bring you food."

"Well, I won't eat it."

"It's not my fault it ended up on the floor. You can lick it up when you get hungry enough." He whirled and started toward the stairs.

Sudden panic rose in me. I believed him: he was going to leave me here, alone, in the dark.

"Did you starve my father, too?" I demanded.

He paused and looked at me over his shoulder. I folded my arms across my chest, resisting the urge to rub my shoulders. I was very cold.

The Beast's eyes narrowed into slits in his fur. "Your arm . . . I didn't realize you were injured. Are you all right?"

I glanced down. My arm felt fine, but it was covered with an impressive amount of dried blood.

"No," I said. "I might be bleeding to death. You need to let me out so someone can take care of my injury."

He opened his mouth wide, his tongue lolling out. I realized it was meant to be a smile.

"You can't keep me here forever," I said.

"Can't I?" The smile vanished, which was something of a relief. "You belong in my pack. It is your nature to be a hunter, and you cannot fight it forever."

My mouth was so dry it took me several seconds to get the words out. "I'm. Not. Yours."

"All the hounds are mine." He leaned closer. "And you know it now. You've let the wildness in you out, you've felt the call of the Hunt. Tell the truth, little sister—have you ever felt truly comfortable among the humans in your village? Did you ever really believe you were one of them? Or did you only feel like your true self when you were in your true shape?"

My heart pounded so hard I felt dizzy. "Don't call me your sister."

He laughed. "Our pack is our family, and you were torn from it by your ancestors' weakness. I should never have let them leave to begin with. I failed in my mission and disappointed my queen. Everything I've done since then, I did to right what went wrong."

" 'Everything I've done,' " I said. "How nice and vague. Why don't we lay out exactly what you've done? You kidnapped people, took them from their families, turned them into animals—"

"They *were* animals," the Beast snarled. "And they were *mine*! They were part of my pack. They had no right to leave me!" He stepped back, his fur bristling, which made him look even larger. "Every person I took *wanted* to be a hound, deep down in their soul. I never stole anyone who hadn't shifted shape first and revealed where they truly belonged. I did them a favor, turning them back. There was wildness in them, and magic, and they had foolishly buried it in human bodies and human minds."

I gripped my elbows with my hands, trying to steady myself. "I don't believe you," I said. "If all you care about is doing what the queen told you, then why do you still have *Darina*? She's not a hound. She never was and never will be. She's got nothing to do with your mission. How are you going to pretend that you're imprisoning *her* for anything other than your own selfish reasons?"

"She is not imprisoned! She can leave whenever she wishes."

"So you've said," I said. "If it's true, let her come tell me herself."

The Beast made a pained sound, low in his throat, and turned away from me. "You know what to do if you get hungry enough."

"Wait!" I said as he started down the stairs.

He glared at me over his shoulder. I tried to think of something else to say. "Um . . . about that book."

"Yes?"

It burned me to let him think that I was relenting,

that I was actually *accepting* something from him. But I forced myself to say, "I would like something to read."

He went still. I was sure that he saw right through me, that he was just going to turn and walk away. Instead he smiled, small and smug. "What sort of books do you like?"

"The sort about killing monsters." I shouldn't have said it, but I couldn't help myself. I wanted that self-satisfied expression gone.

To my surprise, he laughed. Then he turned and left, his tail slicing across the floor before slithering down the stairs after the rest of him.

10

The book the Beast brought me had a picture on its cover of a princess riding a unicorn while fighting a dragon with an (incorrectly held) sword. Just the sort of sop Darina would have liked. I opened it and squinted at the first line—*Princess Pandonisa tossed her long blond hair, refusing to act ladylike*—then shut it.

"I'll need a light to read with," I said.

"I know." He twisted one of the knobs off his candelabra, removing a single candle in a metal holder. He extended it to me.

It was pretty clear that his huge paw wouldn't fit between the bars. I forced myself to reach my hand through and take the candle, trying not to touch his fur or claws. My hand shook so badly that I barely managed to draw the candle into my cell without dropping it.

The Beast smiled again, but there was something sad

in his smile. He stood there for another moment, and I braced myself for whatever he was going to say.

But he simply turned and left. The brush of his fur against the walls sounded like a sigh.

As soon as he was gone, I took the candle to the wall and knelt next to my father's scribbles.

In the candlelight, I could see the words clearly. Some of the letters had been rubbed away, or carved so awkwardly I couldn't make them out, but most of them were clear:

> I am a prisoner of the Beast.
> He wants me to ____ (rubbed out)
> Mirrors
> Change
> Find the rose

Well. That was less helpful than I had been hoping for.

Something whined behind me, and I whirled.

A half-grown pup stood on the landing. He pricked his ears forward—not at me, but at the stew on the floor—and took a cautious step in my direction.

I considered him, then scooped up a clump of the stew and flung it out between the bars.

The pup sprang back, snarling. I stepped away from

the bars, and he approached the stew stiff-legged. He circled it once, sniffing and licking his lips. He looked at me warily. I pretended to look at the wall.

The pup's nostrils flared. He barked at the food several times, as if warning it of his intentions, then backed away as if a piece of the stew might attack him. He looked at me again. I ignored him.

He gathered his legs under him and pounced. He gobbled up a chunky piece, then slid backward across the floor, gulped down what he had in his mouth, and began vigorously scratching his neck with his hind leg, looking studiously innocent.

I placed the candleholder carefully in the corner, making sure the candle remained upright. Then I took another clump of stew—this time, the pup tensed, but didn't move back—and shoved it out through the bars. I backed to the wall.

The pup made a show of hesitating, but he wasn't really. He came at the stew from a diagonal, gulped it down, then sat on his haunches and watched me expectantly.

I took the stew bowl and spilled the rest of it on the floor inside the cell. Then I returned to the far wall, wiping my hands clean on my skirt.

The pup yipped. He tried to stick his muzzle through

the bars, and for a moment I was afraid he would get his head stuck, but he pulled it out. He sniffed the air greedily, licking the side of his mouth.

I held my breath.

The pup batted at the wooden bars with one paw, then eyed the latch. He crouched and leapt, but barely managed to touch the latch with his muzzle. He stepped back, studying the problem, then put both his front paws on one of the bars and stretched his body up as far as it would go. With one of his paws, he batted upward at the latch.

It took him several tries, during which I held my breath, afraid he would give up and go away. But finally, almost by accident, he hit the latch from the correct angle, and it swung up and then fell down against the bars.

The door swung open. He bounced back onto all fours, yelped with enormous pride, and squeezed through the opening into my cell.

I remained where I was, not moving, while he devoured the stew. He'd earned it. Only when he'd licked up the last bit, with intense and noisy concentration, did I get to my feet.

The pup was gone like a shot, dashing out of the cell and streaking up the stairs. I picked up the candle and followed more slowly, my stomach aching and empty.

Too late, I wished I'd kept *some* of the stew inside the bowl.

I hesitated on the landing. I glanced up the stairs, in the direction the pup had gone. That was where the Beast had come from; what had he been doing up there? If I went up, I could find out. . . .

And then what? I wasn't here to find the Beast. I was here to find Darina. If she was up these stairs, she would have heard me by now. Even if she was imprisoned, surely she would have found a way to let me know she was there.

Unless she was bound and gagged . . .

The image made my chest hurt. But it was unlikely; the Beast *had*, weirdly, seemed to care about her comfort.

She was probably somewhere else in the castle. And I didn't know how long I had to find her before the Beast discovered that I had escaped. I couldn't afford to waste any time.

I looked up the stairs, then down, the candlelight barely brushing the darkness in either direction. Finally, I started back down the way I had come.

The stairs wobbled beneath my feet, and I stopped every few seconds to listen for growls or for the whisper of paws on stone, or—worst of all—for laughter. I heard nothing.

Somehow, even the silence felt like a threat.

By the time I reached the door to the dining room, my empty stomach was tied into a knot. I put one hand on the door handle and hesitated, my gut twisting even tighter. Behind that door was the dining room, with its gouged table and steaming feast and the mirror behind the draperies.

Go, my hound. Hunt for me.

All my life, I'd felt the draw of my hound self, of the wildness and fierceness, the addictive thrill of the chase. Sometimes I'd fought it, and sometimes I hadn't. But I'd always believed that when I gave in to it, I was driven by my own inner self. That I was making a choice.

Now I wasn't so sure. If that voice told me to shift, would I? Would my body change against my will? And if I changed again, would I be like the other hounds in this castle? With no ability—and, eventually, no desire—to turn human?

I would race through the room, I decided. I wouldn't even glance at the drapes. If I heard anything, I wouldn't stop, not even for a second.

I pushed the door open.

Warm, humid air hit my face, along with the lush, heady scent of flowers. I stopped short, staring.

This wasn't the dining hall. I was facing a garden, a huge outdoor space filled with greenery and roses. The sun had recently risen—something I hadn't been able to tell from inside my cell—and the morning sunlight gleamed on the roses, sparkling off their every hue: pure white and pale pink, vibrant purple and deep bloodred.

I looked back. Behind me, through the door, was the dim stairwell I had walked down. This *was* the door that should open into the dining hall.

But this was clearly not the dining hall.

It was too late in the year for roses, but the air here was as warm as if it were early summer. Roses filled the space in front of me, their petals luxuriously open, full and beautiful. A narrow path wound its way between the flowers, lined with tiny mosaic cobblestones fitted together in delicate patterns.

Find the rose, my father had scratched into the wall of the cell.

She likes books even better than she likes flowers, the Beast had said.

"Darina?" I called.

No answer. I started down the path. It curved sinuously and then widened into a perfect circle, with stone benches along either side. Between the benches, flowers spilled out of large pots, flat leaves brushing the armrests.

I knelt, putting my face close to one of the roses—a gorgeous mass of fully bloomed petals that were deep pink on the outside and brilliantly yellow in their center. I inhaled their light, summery scents.

Then, to remind myself what I was doing here, I touched the pad of my thumb to one of their tiny numerous thorns.

Three steps later, I stopped to smell another rose—a purple one with a deeper, spicier odor. The mingled smells whirled through me, making me feel oddly light-headed, as if I could get drunk on scents.

I straightened and staggered, then fell sideways, landing hard on my hip. The candle fell, landed on the cobblestones, and sputtered out.

Oops. No *as if* about it.

I got to my hands and knees, feeling oddly like I was about to giggle. A pink rose drooped in front of my face, its outer petals curved in so tightly it looked like the flower was being held in a cup. I reached out and plucked it, breaking the stem with a snap. A thorn bit into my palm, but I barely noticed. I buried my face in the rose. Its smell was lighter than the others', but it filled my head instantly.

Find the rose. But there were hundreds of roses here. How was I supposed to know which one I was looking for?

A sound came through the open door behind me—

the click of claws on stone. It pierced my flower-scented haze, and I dropped the pink rose and scrambled to my feet. But the doorway was still empty.

The scent wound through and around me. But that spark of panic had cleared my head. I didn't know if this rose-haze was a barrier or just some sort of side effect, but either way, I couldn't afford to be overcome by it.

I stepped over the pink rose, which lay sideways across the cobblestones, and strode onward down the path. It ended at a thick wooden door set into a stone wall.

I tried to pull down the handle, even though I already knew it must be locked. To my surprise, the door swung open easily. I stepped through and found myself in the front hall of the castle.

The candles in the sconces and candelabras were now unlit, but slivers of sunlight slashed the walls wherever the narrow, dusty windows let it in. That didn't make much of a difference to the rest of the darkness, which was just as shadowy and impenetrable as it had been at night. I stared around, completely confused, trying to make sense of stairways and directions. I had come into the dining room the first time from the far end . . . but surely that meant the *front* end of the castle was behind me? Or was it to the side? How was I back under the balcony? How had I gotten here?

A laugh echoed against the stones, low and delighted and predatory.

I backed out of the door again, into the garden, then turned and ran down the path the other way, paying no attention to the roses this time. There, at the other end, was another door—the one I had stepped through after going down the stairs. I wrenched it open.

But there was no stairway there. I was in the main entrance hall again.

Dizziness swirled through me as my mind tried to make sense of my location. For a second, I was afraid I would fall. I kept a tight grip on the door handle until the feeling passed, then slammed the door shut and stepped back into the rose garden.

Not that I had any reason to think the garden was safe. But at least here, nothing was laughing at me.

Then I looked at the door I had just closed and saw that there was a mirror attached to the back of it—a rectangular strip of reflective glass that had been nailed right down its center. I was staring into my own wide, frightened eyes.

I stepped back, and my reflection vanished. The mirror filled with the image of a single, dying rose. It drooped in a crystal flowerpot, atop a gigantic stem studded with thorns and dripping with leaves. It looked like it was glowing, even though it was pathetically ugly; there was no flower at its top, just a thorny little stump from which drooped long, withered leaves and a single limp red petal.

A hand reached into the frame and touched that remaining petal. Just a hand, slender and graceful, but with a familiar mole near the thumb and incongruously ragged fingernails. Darina had never managed to break her habit of biting her nails.

"Darina!" I shouted, and reached for her.

My fingers went right through the mirror's glass. It felt cool and liquid, like I was pushing through a current. My fingers brushed something velvety, and then a sharp point pierced my thumb. I snatched my hand back with a gasp.

There was a drop of blood on the pad of my thumb. I put it into my mouth and smelled something faintly flowery coming off my skin. The image of the rose vanished, and I found myself staring again at my own face, grimy and rumpled.

Then I saw Darina's face behind my reflection, her eyes wide with astonishment.

"Darina?" I stepped forward again, tensed for my hand to go through the glass. But this time, my fingertips pressed against the mirror's cold, unyielding surface, and went no farther.

"Argh!" I said in frustration, and Darina's hand went to her lips.

"What are you *doing*, Mera?"

Her voice didn't come from the mirror. It came from behind me.

I whirled.

My sister stood in the garden, in the center of the cobblestone path, staring at me in astonishment.

11

Darina looked completely unharmed. She looked, in fact, more beautiful than ever. She was wearing an elaborate yellow gown made of finer silk than I'd ever seen, with ruffles lining the sleeves and neckline. Her hair was coiled in braids around her face, which had grown thinner since I'd last seen her—but somehow, instead of making her look gaunt, the thinness just accentuated her fine bones and the largeness of her eyes.

I stood there staring at her, not moving, and it took me a moment to realize why: because I didn't believe she was really there. Any moment now, she would vanish, and I would hear that malicious laughter tinkling through the air.

"Get away from the mirror," Darina said. "The mirrors here are dangerous! Honestly, Mera, don't you ever stop to *think*—"

I threw myself across the space between us and

collided into her, wrapping my arms around her waist. Darina staggered back and grunted. Then her arms came up and she hugged me back.

We remained like that for what felt like a long time, and like no time at all. I squeezed her with every bit of strength I had, as if it might be possible to never let go. As if I had just woken from a nightmare and only Darina could make me feel safe.

We weren't safe. I knew that. But we were alive, and we were together, and that meant the worst was over. We would get out of this castle. We could go to our father, and he would take us far away, to somewhere across the sea where even the Beast could never follow us.

"What are you doing here?" Darina pushed me away, first gently and then—when I wouldn't budge—more firmly. Her face was streaked with delicate lines of tears. "I'm so glad to see you, Mera—I missed you—but you shouldn't have come. This castle can be treacherous if you don't know how to get around it."

"I noticed that." I was crying, too—which, I knew without looking at the mirror, had turned *my* face into a blotchy mess—but I was laughing at the same time. "If I had known how awful it was, I would have come sooner. I'm sorry, it was my fault, and I've been looking and *looking* for you, but then the Beast—and there was something behind the mirror, and I got trapped in this garden, and then the mirror showed me a dying rose—"

Darina's hands tightened on my shoulders. "A rose?"

"Yes, in the mirror—and I thought I saw your hand—and there was this, this *laughing* person—" I turned and gestured at the rectangular mirror, afraid of what I would see in it. But all I saw was my own face, blotchy as expected, and Darina with her hand pressed to her mouth.

"You saw a dying rose in the mirror?" she said. "You're sure?"

I forced myself to stop babbling. "Listen, Darina. I don't know where the Beast is—he thinks I'm still in a cage—and that door opens to the front hall. At least it did last time I opened it. This is our chance. We have to go—"

"No." She dropped her hands and stepped away from me. "No, Mera. I can't."

"You can! I have a plan." *Plan* was a wild exaggeration, but I plunged on. "We have to leave this village entirely. Get to the port, get on a ship, start a new life. There's no other way. Father will help us, and I'll come with you, and Grandma—" I hesitated. It was impossible to imagine Grandma leaving her home and getting on a ship to an unknown land. "We'll make sure Grandma knows what we're doing. As long as she knows we're safe, she'll be all right."

Was that true? I wasn't at all sure that was true. But neither of us could stay, not now that the Beast knew what I was. He would take us both back no matter what we wanted, unless we did something drastic and took ourselves out of his reach.

Darina bit her lip. "You don't understand. I didn't— the Beast didn't kidnap me. I came here, I—" She twisted her hands together. "I'm so sorry. I should have left a note, but I didn't know where Grandma had put the ink, and I wasn't thinking clearly ..."

"I know," I said. "It's all right. I know you came to save Father. We'll talk about it later—"

"I was woken in the middle of the night by a hound howling outside my window." Apparently, we were going to talk about it now. "But when I looked out, there was no hound. There was only a note on our windowsill. It said, *Your father is imprisoned in the Beast's castle. Only you can free him. Come at once.* So of course I went."

"Of course." I sighed. "How did you get into the castle?"

"He knew I would come. The front door of the castle opened for me as I was walking up to it. Then the candles in the front hall all came alight, even though there was no one there to light them." She shuddered. "And then ... then the Beast came. I told him why I was there and begged him to let Father go. He said, *You are very brave, human girl.*"

"Really? Not, *You're the wrong sister, I wanted the other one?*"

Darina looked at me blankly, as if she couldn't make sense of my words. "I thought he would put me in a cage. Instead, he gave me a grand room. I was free to roam the castle. He brought me food and everything I needed. Even books from his library."

"Books!" I exclaimed. "How generous of him."

"We started to talk—about what I was reading, about my life, about *his* life. He's nothing like what I expected, Mera. He's gentle, deep down, and so terribly sad. First the Faerie Queen trapped him in this life, and then his hounds abandoned him, and he was just ... stuck. Stuck and alone, for so long. His loneliness led him to do terrible things, but that's not who he truly is. He's sorry for what he's done to our village."

This conversation was going in a direction I hadn't imagined. I could barely understand what she was saying. "Is he?" I asked. "Because people who are sorry for things don't usually keep right on doing them. I'm only here because I escaped from the cell he locked me in!"

Darina drew back. "That's ... I'm sorry. How awful. When he saw you, he must have panicked—"

"He didn't panic," I said. "He knew exactly what he was doing. He *told* me. He didn't want me to talk to you.

He wants to make sure you only talk to *him*, because that way he can convince you he's kind and gentle and ... and has great taste in books, and ... he can control you—"

"He doesn't want to control me!" Darina said.

"Sure. That's why he kidnapped you and kept you trapped in a castle."

"It's not that simple. He doesn't want to hurt people, or to be hated. He wants ..." She drew in her breath. "He wants to change. He wants to be human."

"I don't think so," I said. "He seemed pretty committed to re-creating his pack."

"He was." Darina's blush darkened. "He never wanted to be human before. But he does now."

I knew then what she was trying to tell me. I knew, but it was so unbelievable I didn't know I knew. "Why?"

"For me," Darina said. "He's fallen in love with me, and I with him. He wants to be human so we can get married."

I stepped back. The air around me felt thick and suffocating, the scent of the roses suddenly sickening. We stared at each other in absolute silence.

The silence was broken by a roar, and then by Darina's shriek, and then by a deafening thud as the Beast burst through the door, his misshapen shadow darkening the roses and falling over the two of us.

12

For a moment I wondered if the Beast had been listening outside the door, waiting for the most dramatic possible moment to rush in.

But only for a moment, because the Beast was clearly too angry to have waited for so long as a single second. His eyes were blazing, his face screwed up in rage. Among the exquisite, delicate roses, with the sunlight mercilessly illuminating his malformed features, he looked even more grotesque than he had in the dark stairwell. He roared again, in pure, violent rage, and lunged at me.

There was no intelligence, no sign of the earlier humanity or sadness in his eyes. I heard myself scream as if from a distance, and I squeezed my eyes shut.

Then I heard another shout, lower and weaker.

"*Stop!* Don't touch her!"

"Darina!" My eyes popped open. "No!"

My sister had thrown herself between me and the Beast. She was a quarter his size, but she faced him squarely, her chin lifted.

The Beast stopped.

The rage on his face didn't diminish, but he stopped. His huge front claw froze midswing, inches from Darina's fragile body.

"*Move,*" he snarled.

My sister said, "No."

He could have killed her with one swipe of that deadly claw. But he didn't. He howled, reached up in fury, and yanked at the thick ruff around his neck. Clumps of his fur scattered to the ground. One landed on my face and made me sneeze.

I immediately wished I hadn't. The Beast turned his glare on me.

"You shouldn't be here!" he shouted. The thunder of his voice made the nearby roses quiver. "How dare you harm my flowers?"

I could hear Darina's shallow, rapid breathing. Fragments of fur drifted down, settling on the rose petals. The Beast bared his teeth.

"She wasn't harming the flowers!" Darina said. "She was searching for me."

"He knows exactly what I'm doing." I got to my feet, pulling myself straight, trying to pretend I hadn't just been crouching on the ground with my arms over my head. I was shaking all over, including my voice. "I explained it all to him while he was keeping me in a cage. He told me that if you got to talk to me, it would *ruin everything*. His words."

The Beast shrank back—just a bit, but it made hope swell in my chest. I grabbed Darina's hand. "Don't you see? He's tricked you. He's kept you prisoner so long you can't think straight, and that's why he's trying to keep me away from you."

She wrenched her hand free and stepped toward the Beast. "My sister's not going to ruin anything. She's going to save us!" She beamed up at him. "She's seen the fae rose!"

"What?" The Beast's head swung toward me. "The dying rose? The one with only one petal left? You saw it?"

"Um . . ." I wanted to deny it. But I had already told Darina the truth. "Maybe?"

"You did see it." His eyes went alight. "This means there is hope for me yet."

"Hope for *what*?" I demanded.

He turned to me, his yellow eyes glowing. "A long time ago, I tried to become human. My pack had abandoned me, the humans feared me, and finally, in my weakness, I gave in to temptation. I tried to change."

He gestured at himself, his face grim. "As you can see, it didn't work."

I stared at him, suddenly seeing his monstrous body for what it was. The squashed muzzle, the long fingers that ended in claws, the heavy, furry arms . . . "It wasn't the queen who transformed you. You used to be a hound. You got stuck in the middle of the change."

"Yes." He shuddered all over, a loud ruffle of fur. "I don't know why. Perhaps the queen's charge lay heaviest on me, or perhaps there was not enough of the rose left. I nearly died in the attempt—I kept trying to complete the change, even as I felt my strength giving out. I did not even manage to consume the whole rose before I lost consciousness. When I woke, the rose was gone, and I was . . . this."

Darina looked like she was about to burst into tears. This, no doubt, was one of the sob stories the Beast had fed her while keeping her imprisoned.

As the Beast was about to find out, I was not as susceptible as Darina. I folded my arms across my chest. "I'll feel very sorry for you once I'm far away from you."

"I tried to find the remnants of the last rose," he went on, as if I hadn't spoken. "But the castle had hidden it from me. Then I tried to regrow the queen's gift, hoping that something in the soil would turn regular roses into the kind of flower I needed." He gestured at the garden.

"Nothing worked. My frustration grew and twisted and consumed me. Before long, all I could think of was re-creating what should have been mine." He hesitated. "I believed it was right. I had no reason to think otherwise. I told myself I was fulfilling my mission, but in truth . . . in truth I was just lonely." He met Darina's eyes. "It is easier to see that clearly, now that I am not lonely anymore."

Darina blushed, her eyelashes sweeping down across her cheeks.

"That's a very pretty speech," I said. "But . . ."

Darina turned to me and grabbed my hands. "Don't you see, Mera? If you can find the lost rose, he could complete his transformation! He could turn human!"

"He doesn't want to be human," I snapped. I turned to the Beast, which at that moment felt easier than talking to Darina. "What about all the wildness in you and the call of the Hunt and the blah blah blah of the pack?"

He didn't even look at me. He kept smiling down at Darina. "Love is stronger than any of those."

Two days ago, if someone had told me I would find the Beast *sappy*, I would have laughed in their face. I didn't feel like laughing now. "Anyhow, who said I can *find* the rose? I just saw it. Briefly. In passing."

"That still means something," the Beast said. "The mirrors have never shown me the rose, and your sister can't see through the mirrors at all—she likes what she sees when she looks into a mirror. They will only show her reflections. But you and I . . ."

I flinched. "I'm not like you!" I said. "I'm not hideous!"

I was ashamed of myself as soon as I said it. But a small, mean part of me also wanted to see him flinch.

Instead, he laughed. "No, you're not. I don't know why *you* can see through the reflections. But it seems you can." He tilted his head to one side. "Why don't you like what the mirror shows you?"

"I'm not going to discuss that. Not with *you*." My face burned. I felt a faint, shrinking shame wash over me, the familiar sense that there was something about me that was inadequate.

Usually, when that happened, I reminded myself that I was different from the people judging me. That I had a secret—a wild, fierce side that they didn't know about.

I couldn't do that now.

Instead, I reminded myself that the Beast was evil, that I hated him, and that I was not going to be made to feel lesser by *him*. I curled my lip. "It doesn't matter. Even if I *could* find you your rose, why would I do anything to help you? You kidnapped my father and my sister, you put me in a cage—"

"You put yourself in a cage," he pointed out.

"—*kept* me in a cage, and now you're asking for favors?"

"I'll take you through the castle," he said. "We'll look

in each mirror. There are many, but I know where they all are. All you have to do is tell me which one shows you the rose. I'll go through the mirror myself and retrieve it."

"I don't think so," I said. "Find your own rose."

The Beast drew his lips back in a snarl. Darina put a hand on his furry arm.

"Please, Mera," she said. "For me."

I didn't want to look at her. But there didn't seem to be another alternative, so I turned my head just far enough to give her a side-glare. "It's not for you. You're only asking because he wants you to! He's controlling you."

"No," the Beast said. "Only my hounds are under my control. I cannot force your sister to do anything she doesn't want to do."

"You manipulated her into wanting it! You held her prisoner and confused her into forgetting that you're a monster." I narrowed my eyes. "Well, I'm here to remind her."

The Beast's eyes flashed. "You forget," he snarled. "I can't control your sister, but I can control *you*."

I lifted my chin. "I'm not one of your hounds."

"Aren't you?" He rose to his full height. His thick arms hung past his knees, each wickedly curved claw larger than my head. "Come, little sister. Take your true form."

His voice washed over me, an inescapable command.

I opened my mouth, but no words came out—no words *could* come out of a muzzle. I spent a split second choking on the attempt, and then I snarled. I had never changed so fast before; though my body was now a hound's, my four paws planted on the ground and my tail lashing, my thoughts were still human.

Darina made a low, strangled sound, and through my panic I felt a flash of triumph. The Beast had made a mistake. He was deluded if he thought he could hurt me in front of my sister and still keep her from seeing him for what he was.

His face clenched as he realized it. He looked at Darina, his shoulders hunching together. "It won't hurt her," he said. "She's changed into a hound before on her own, many times."

"I know," Darina said.

I snapped my teeth together in shock.

"I've known for a while," she said to me. She stepped closer to the Beast. "But, Beast, you can't—I know you're angry, but please—"

"She could free me!" the Beast roared at her. Darina cringed back, and so, instinctively, did I. "She could end my suffering, she could fix everything for both of us! All I'm asking her to do is *look*. If she truly loved you, she would do it for your sake."

"She just needs time!" Darina pleaded. "Let me talk to her. I can convince her. . . ."

Her voice trailed off. Darina had never been able to convince me of anything.

"She won't do it for you," the Beast spat. "So let her do it for herself." He turned and glared at me, and I scrambled back, whimpering. "You want your human body back? Get me the rose. When I turn human, so will all my hounds. Including you."

I wished I was brave enough to growl at him, but my human self was too terrified, and it was unthinkable to my hound self. I tucked my tail between my legs.

Darina crossed the floor and knelt in front of me. She put one hand on the side of my muzzle. Tears spilled over her lashes and down her cheeks.

"Please, Mera," she said. "I know you don't understand, but I promise, this is the right thing to do. He needs the rose. Please help us."

I wasted another moment trying to make my muzzle form words—I had so, so many of them—before I settled for growling. I grabbed her sleeve in my teeth and tugged.

Darina met my eyes, and I tried to put my words into my gaze: *Come with me. Get away from him. Let's go.*

She tugged her sleeve free. She stepped back, and

back again, until she was at the Beast's side. She lifted her hand, and his huge claw engulfed it.

A strangled, choked sound filled the garden, and I realized I had made it.

"Just help us," Darina said. Her words came out between sobs. "Please. Why do you always have to be so difficult?"

I couldn't reply, of course. I could only snarl. But I found that I couldn't even do that.

Luckily, I also couldn't cry.

I turned and ran. Through the door, into the great hall, over the stones, beneath the unlit candles. The front door was open, and I raced through it without pausing or looking back.

But I was a hound; I couldn't stop being aware of my surroundings. So even as I kept my gaze fixed firmly ahead, I could hear and smell the absence behind me.

And I knew that neither my sister nor the Beast was coming after me.

13

I raced through the woods in hound form, splashing through the creek, weaving between the trees. I didn't stop my headlong flight until I reached the village. Then, finally, I slowed down, my muscles aching and my fur ruffled by the wind.

I thought about trying to shift back to human, but only for a second. I knew the Beast hadn't been bluffing.

He was exactly what he had always been. He would trap me in the form he preferred without a second thought. That wasn't even surprising.

But Darina hadn't protected me. She had stood by his side and watched him do it.

Just help us, she'd said to me.

I would never help them. Never. The Beast could rage and threaten all he wanted. I would remain a hound forever before I looked for his precious rose.

I crept carefully around the village inn and tavern,

staying downwind from the stables. The back door of the tavern opened suddenly, and I froze in the trees, watching as Ressa and Talya came out together, carrying a slop bucket between them. Ressa and Talya's parents owned the inn, and the whole family lived and worked there. Talya liked to boast about her cooking skills and to regale the village children with stories she'd heard from exotic travelers. Somehow, she had neglected to mention that hauling stinky garbage was one of her duties.

If I ever turned human again, I would have to find just the right time to bring that up, in front of as many people as possible.

Talya and Ressa tugged the bucket to the edge of the trees and dumped it just yards from where I was hiding. It spread over the ground with surprising speed, a mass of food waste and dishwater, and I stepped back. A twig cracked under my paw, and Ressa turned sharply. For a moment, she was as still as I was.

"Come *on*," Talya said. "Let's get back inside. You promised you'd do my hair."

Ressa blinked into the trees, straight at me. Then she twitched her shoulder, hefted the empty bucket, and followed Talya back inside.

I waited until the door closed behind them. Then I kept going.

The sun was higher in the sky now, but it was early enough that few people were out and about, and there were still enough shadows to hide in for a creature as silent and graceful as me. I slunk carefully along the village streets, alert to all sounds and smells. Ahead of me, the milkman was starting his rounds, and I switched my route to avoid him. There was an intriguing pile of sewage collecting in a hollow spot, and my hound self wanted to sniff and investigate, but I loped by without stopping. My human self wanted only to get home, to find Grandma and show her what had happened to me. She had known for years what I could become; she had dealt with it calmly, the first time I changed, and told me where my ability came from and what I could do to stay safe. She would be disappointed that I hadn't followed her instructions, but she would help me.

She *could* help me, no matter what the Beast thought about his powers.

On a side street, a small shape slunk through the same shadows I was keeping to: the baker's cat had gotten out again. I avoided that street, too. There was only so much temptation a pup could be expected to withstand.

It all went smoothly until I got close to my own house. My hound's ears could make out the sound of angry voices all the way from the bottom of the street. I crouched, bristling.

"—not my fault!" That was my father; I had nearly forgotten how strident his bellows were, and how far they carried. "If you had told me from the beginning—"

My grandmother cut him off. She, too, was impressively loud. "You should have come here right away. As soon as you were free, you should have left that castle—"

"And left my daughter alone with the Beast? I stayed to protect her!"

"A fine job you've done of it."

"At least I tried! You *knew* this might happen, and you chose to just sit in your rocking chair knitting and hoping everything would work out somehow!"

"I don't *knit*," Grandma said icily. "I crochet. And everything *would* have worked out if you hadn't gone to the castle in the first place!"

"What choice did I have?"

"Would you like me to make you a list?"

"Sure, if that will keep you busy while I go back—"

My grandmother cut him off. This time, her voice was low and dangerous, and I couldn't make out the words.

Judging from her tone, that was probably a good thing.

"I *am* going back!" That was my father again. "I won't lose *both* my daughters to that creature. I won't."

I didn't wait to hear what Grandma said in response. I leapt from the ground, earth spurting up behind my paws, and raced toward home without any attempt at stealth.

"Grandma!" I shouted. It came out as a yelp.

I gathered myself as I ran. The shutters of the kitchen window were open, and while that window was too small for a full-grown hound, a pup like me should be able to make it through.

I waited until I was right beneath the window, and then I leapt straight up. My front paws barely touched the sill, my tail brushed the wall, and I was through. I landed lightly on the kitchen floor, right next to the table where my grandmother and father were sitting.

Well, where they *had* been sitting. By the time I landed they were both on their feet and screaming a *lot* louder than they had been before.

My father reached for the knife at his belt. He had it drawn back to throw before Grandma grabbed his arm.

"Stop!" she shouted. "What are you doing?"

The knife clattered to the floor. My father stared at me. The smell of his fear was so strong it drowned out anything else he might have been feeling.

"Darina?" he whispered.

Seriously? I shook out my fur and glared at him.

Grandma let go of my father's arm, and he dropped back into his chair. My grandmother bent slowly, one hand on her lower back, and retrieved his knife from the floor. She placed it on the table, then turned to me.

"Can you shift back?" she asked.

I whined.

She sighed. "Well, that's a problem. Are you hurt?"

"She has blood on her fur," my father said, and then I recognized what I was smelling from him. Not fear. Disgust.

I twisted and carefully licked the blood off my hind-quarters. It was only a tiny patch. I wasn't even sure how it had gotten there.

Grandma's brow furrowed. She knelt so her eyes were level with mine. "Why are you in this form, Mera?"

The answer to that was far too complicated to manage without human speech. In fact, I wasn't sure how well I would manage *with* human speech. I padded across the kitchen to Grandma's wooden medicine chest, nudged it with my nose, and looked at her.

She straightened—with my hound's ears, I could actually hear her bones creaking—and crossed the room to me. She opened the chest.

Flowery, spicy, and bitter scents immediately flooded the room. I stuck my nose into the chest. Grandma swatted me away and drew out a small glass bottle. My hound's vision didn't distinguish between colors the way my human eyes would have, but I knew the powder in it was the same gray-pink as the powder in my pouch.

Carefully, Grandma unstoppered the bottle and scattered a tiny bit of powder on the floor.

"What is that?" my father asked.

"Ground-up petals from one of the original fae roses." My grandmother eyed the powder on the floor, looked me over, then added another pinch. "My great-great-great-grandmother made it, and our family has always kept it on hand. This bottle is all that's left." She put the stopper back. "There you go, Mera. That should be enough."

But she didn't put the bottle back yet. She held it, watching me.

I found myself hesitating. Once I was back in human form, everything was going to be so difficult. That feeling that had come over me, when Darina had stepped away from me and taken the Beast's claw, would come again and pull me under a wave of anguish. As a hound, I could remember her betrayal, I could even be angry about it, but it didn't *hurt* the way it would once I was human again.

What if I didn't shift back? Not yet, anyhow. What if I rushed right out the door and into the woods?

My muscles bunched together. Grandma drew in her breath, as if she knew what I was going to do, but that didn't matter. She couldn't stop me. No one could stop me. I turned my head toward the door, every limb of my body quivering.

Then I remembered the Beast saying *I can control you. Take your true form.*

I bent my head and licked up the powder with one swipe of my tongue.

The taste exploded inside my mouth, and there was nothing flowery about it. Sharp bitterness burned my tongue and then my throat. I leapt back, swiping at my muzzle with my front paw.

The burning sensation spread through my body. It was like the change was being stretched out and re-sisted, so that what usually happened too fast to feel was instead spread over several long, uncomfortable moments. My bones screamed in pain, my skin tingled savagely, and the world went black. I snarled and shook my head, trying to scrape at my skin with my paws.

And then, finally, the tingling faded.

I tried to get to my feet—and discovered, to my dismay, that I was already on my feet. All four of them. I stared down at my paws, then looked up at my grandmother.

"Hmm," she said. "That's concerning."

I pointed my muzzle at the bottle she was holding.

"No," she said. "More rose powder won't help. I already gave you twice as much as you should have needed." She tapped her foot against the floor. "Were you hunting last night?"

I barked.

"With a pack?"

I barked again.

"What difference does that make?" my father demanded. Now I could smell both his fear and his disgust, so mixed together he probably couldn't tell the difference between them.

"The hounds are part of the Wild Hunt," my grandmother said. "That's their true purpose, their reason for being in this world. The closer she gets to the essence of her hound self, the harder it's going to be for her to shift back to human. It's not her fault."

My father snorted. "That sounds like it's exactly her fault."

Had I been human, the question of whose fault it was might have seemed very relevant. Also, the prospect of being stuck in hound form might have frightened me, and the fact that my father knew what I was might have humiliated me. Instead, a deep sense of calm welled up in me.

"Mera didn't know this would happen," my grandmother said.

"Then it's *your* fault," my father snapped. "Why didn't you tell her?"

My grandmother drew herself up, eyes flashing.

"And what does this mean for her?" my father asked quickly. "Is she going to be a hound forever now, like the others the Beast has turned?"

They both looked at me. I tucked my tail between my legs.

"No," my grandmother said. "Not after only a single Hunt. She'll probably be able to shift back after she gets some sleep."

Probably?

"The castle was full of hounds," my father said, "and I never saw one take human form. *They* can't shift."

"Being near the Beast makes it harder," Grandma said. "He's the pack leader, and it's difficult for hounds to break away from a pack. Besides, they've all been hounds for decades at least, and they've forgotten what it is to be human. Mera hasn't gotten to that point. Yet." She put the bottle back and closed the medicine chest. "I think it would do all of us good to get some rest."

I started toward the stairs. She looked at me sternly. "You sleep in the kitchen. I don't need to be cleaning fur out of the blankets now, on top of everything else."

I sat down on the cold stone floor. There was a certain tone my grandmother used that was impossible to argue with. Or to growl at.

(I did bare my teeth, but only once she was upstairs.)

My father looked at me like he was going to say something. (He, too, had waited until Grandma was upstairs.) Before he could, I put my muzzle on my front paws and closed my eyes.

After several seconds, I heard the door open and then shut behind him.

I rolled over and flopped onto the floor, squeezing my eyes shut and stretching my legs out. I wondered if I would ever again have only two legs. Already, it was hard to imagine being human; this form felt so *right*.

My grandmother had sounded confident that I could shift back eventually, but she didn't know that it was the Beast's command that had changed me. I could still feel that command thrumming through my bones. I knew my human self would be outraged by it, but to the hound, it was perfectly natural to be commanded by the pack's master. It was hard to remember why I would want to fight that command.

Maybe *trapped* was just a state of mind. If I didn't feel trapped, then I wasn't. If I never wanted to switch back, then I wouldn't. I would hunt with my pack and run in the woods and never be bothered by human concepts like loyalty and betrayal. I would be fierce and free and wild forever.

It would be so easy. All I had to do was stay in this form. *My* form.

But then what would happen to Darina?

If I had been human, I doubt I'd have been able to fall asleep at all. Luckily, hounds don't have such problems.

14

When I woke, I was still a hound. I stretched, yawned widely, then rolled over onto my back and spent a few seconds scratching my head with my front paws.

I had discovered something interesting during my nap: dogs dream. In the dream I had been running with a pack, hunting something large and dangerous, paws digging into the snow. There was a primal cruelty running through me, the knowledge that our prey would not escape, that the pounding of our paws was bringing us closer, that we would bring it down. Its panic was sweet, its heavy, frantic breathing a song.

So dogs don't dream very *imaginatively*. Still, I woke feeling like I should be running, my muscles still twitching and my mouth watering.

I did not feel at all like I wanted to be a human girl.

The kitchen was small and confining and far too warm. Though it did smell like something appetizing . . .

I rolled back over, shook myself, and scratched industriously below my ear with one of my back paws. Late-afternoon sunlight slanted through the windows, making dust motes dance in front of my eyes. My grandmother was at the stove, stirring a pot of porridge. I got to my feet and padded over.

"I'd imagine you missed breakfast," she said, not looking up from her stirring. "There's a bowl and spoon on the table. Change into a form in which you can use them."

I growled low—too low for her to hear—and went reluctantly to the table. I could smell traces of my father's scent from this morning, but nothing fresher than that. He hadn't come back.

I shook my fur out. I felt perfectly content, at home in my skin; there was nothing on my mind but food and the Hunt. And my pack. If I changed back to human, a mass of confusing emotions would crash down on me . . . emotions that I remembered but didn't fully understand, except that I knew they weren't good.

Why would I plunge myself back into that morass when I could stay in my current form? The form I had always been meant to have.

My stomach grumbled. The porridge smelled delicious, and I was hungry.

"Go on," Grandma said. "You've been away from the Beast for hours now. His power over you will have faded."

Her voice was nonchalant, but I could smell her tension. She wanted me to change, and she was afraid that I couldn't.

Or that I wouldn't.

In the end, it wasn't the porridge that made up my mind. It was that I had a lot of questions, and no way to ask them as a hound.

I braced for failure as I reached for my human self. But the tingling went through me immediately, the familiar half-pain as my limbs stretched and altered. I reached for another part of me, a part that had been hidden away in an inaccessible place, and traded it for the self I was currently showing the world.

My grandmother kept her back to me, which I appreciated; even though the change always brought me back fully clothed, there was something about it that felt private. She didn't speak until I had taken a seat at the table and picked up a spoon.

Then she said, "I gather you've been doing this frequently."

Her voice snapped on the last word, which was when I realized how furious she was.

Grandma turned around, holding the stirring spoon

like she wanted to stab someone with it. I pushed my chair back.

(I'm not saying my grandmother would have stabbed me. But I *was* the only person around . . .)

"How long," she demanded, "have you been running around as a hound?"

"I haven't been *running around*," I protested. "Just . . . occasionally. Almost never. A few nights a year."

"You were planning to shift into a hound in broad daylight just yesterday, before your father showed up!"

How did she know that? It seemed like the wrong time to ask. "That was an exception. I was trying to help Darina. And no one saw me! I stayed deep in the forest, I didn't hurt anyone—"

"You hurt *yourself*!" Grandma twisted and slammed the spoon into the pot with such force that porridge splattered upward. When she started toward me, she had a blob of porridge stuck to the edge of her right eyebrow. Somehow, it didn't make her look any less intimidating. "What did I tell you the first time you changed?"

I recited it back to her. "To never do it again. To take a pouch filled with rose powder with me everywhere, and eat some if I felt the change starting. Because otherwise I might get stuck in the shape of a hound."

"Is that what you want? To be a hound forever?"

"No! Of course not!" I could hear my voice not sounding entirely convincing. "But that's not going to happen."

She looked pointedly at the hearth, where I had slept for the past few hours with my muzzle tucked against my side.

"I never got stuck before." I put the spoon down and crossed my arms over my chest. It was pretty obvious that I was wrong, and I hated being wrong. It made my next words belligerent. "It wasn't *my* fault. It's because of the Beast. He made me shift. He has power over his hounds."

"Yes," Grandma said. "He does. He's the master of the Hunt." She was still for a moment, her face tight. Then she walked the rest of the way to the table, pulled out the chair across from mine, and sat.

So she wasn't going to serve the porridge, apparently. My stomach grumbled.

Grandma looked down. For a hopeful moment, I thought she was focusing on my empty bowl. But her eyes hadn't dropped that far. She was looking at my rose-powder pouch, which was dangling outside my blouse.

I reached for it reflexively. I had never opened it or looked inside it, not since the very first time Grandma had given it to me. When Darina had asked me what was in it, I had told her it was a good-luck charm that could never be opened. She'd rolled her eyes scornfully, but

I had stuck to my story. It was the one secret Grandma had ever told only to me.

I let the pouch thud against my chest. "I've never needed the rose powder before."

"No," Grandma said. "Not until you let yourself be discovered by the Beast. Now he will lure you into his pack, and you will be whatever he wants you to be. I tried to tell you. Being wild is not the same as being free."

I looked down. "I'm sorry."

She sighed. "I understand the temptation, Mera. I do."

She didn't. But I kept my mouth shut and my eyes down, and then my stomach chose that moment to rumble loudly. Grandma pursed her lips. "I guess I had better feed you."

I wasn't going to argue with that. Grandma got to her feet, supporting herself on the table, and made her way across the kitchen.

Something thudded against the front door.

My grandmother turned, just a few feet from the porridge pot. (So close!) She started across the room toward the door.

She was almost there when the door swung open. The half-grown pup who had released me from my cell bounded into the kitchen. He made a beeline straight for me, put both his paws on my chair, then leapt onto my lap. He sniffed at my bowl and, finding it empty, twisted to look at me with wide-eyed despair.

I laughed. For a moment, I even forgot my hunger. "Hey there. How did you find me? And how on earth did you come to the conclusion that *I'm* a reliable source of food?" The pup barked, and I looked up at Grandma. "This pup is from—"

But Grandma wasn't looking at me. She took two steps toward the half-open door.

I saw what she had a moment later. Darina stumbled into the doorway, wearing her fancy yellow gown, her hair in bead-strewn strands over her shoulders. She took one step forward, then collapsed onto the kitchen floor.

15

I moved more quickly than I had known I was capable of, spilling the pup onto the floor. He fell over on his back with his paws scrabbling in the air, then wiggled over and shook himself, trying to pretend that nothing undignified had happened.

My grandmother was even faster than I was. By the time I reached Darina, Grandma had already turned her onto her side.

"Get a damp cloth," she barked at me. "And pull the medicine chest over."

I obeyed. When I reached Grandma with the medicine chest, Darina was stirring, struggling to get up. That seemed like the right time to press the damp cloth to her forehead. But she knocked it away with a scowl.

"Stop, Mera! You're dripping water into my eyes! I'm *fine*."

"Is the Beast following you?" I demanded.

"No." She sat up. "I told him I wanted to see you, and he said I should go."

I had a quick flashback to the Beast glaring at me through the bars: *She's mine now.*

"He set you free?" I repeated. "Why?"

"It's a long story." She pushed herself to her hands and knees, then stood cautiously, swaying the tiniest bit. "And I'm really hungry."

So finally, we got porridge.

Darina had devoured three bowls full, and I was half-way through my second, before Grandma's patience ran out. She put her spoon down with a clang that was loud enough to make me jump. "Darina. Explain. What happened to you in the castle? How did you escape? Is the Beast going to come after you?"

Darina licked the last bit of porridge from her spoon, then put it down reluctantly. I put my spoon down, too, less reluctantly. I had gone with remarkable speed from feeling like I wanted to eat everything in sight, to feeling like I was about to throw up and then never eat again.

Something cold nudged my leg. I glanced down, and the pup looked at me soulfully. I put my bowl on the floor and he attacked it enthusiastically.

"The Beast is not coming after me," Darina said. My heart leapt, and then she added, "He has no reason to. I'm going back to the castle. I just . . . I wanted to see you first." Her eyes skittered over my face, and she looked back at her bowl. "I wanted to explain."

My chest felt tight. "Explain why you pretended to be in love with the Beast?"

Grandma looked up sharply. Darina picked her spoon back up and turned it over in her hand. "I wasn't pretending. We've been wrong about him. He's not a monster at all. He never hurt me or mistreated me—"

"He did mistreat *me*," I broke in. "Maybe you don't care, but I think Grandma should know. He locked me in a cell, he forced me to become a hound—"

"That's only because—"

"Of his deep pain and loneliness. Yes, yes, I've heard."

She glared at me. I glared back. We both turned to look at our grandmother.

Grandma sat completely still, her face fixed in a weirdly blank expression. The silence stretched.

"I hope you can be happy for me," Darina said finally. "But if you're not, it won't make a difference. The Beast and I belong together. I don't care what anyone else thinks."

It didn't sound at all believable. Darina was not very good at defiance. She was so used to being admired that even mild disapproval was unbearable to her.

I tried to speak levelly. "You've been under the Beast's

control for more than three months. Maybe you should spend a little more time thinking about it on your own before you go marry him? Stay here for a few months..." Her eyes narrowed, and I said hastily, "Or a few weeks. See how you feel then."

"I can't stay away that long," she said. "The Beast will miss me too much."

I whirled away from her. "Grandma, talk to her!"

Grandma was staring at Darina's hand. On Darina's finger was a white-gold ring with a pink quartz stone shaped like a flower.

"Where did you get that?" Grandma demanded.

Darina curled her fingers together protectively. "The Beast gave it to me."

The pup scrambled onto my lap. He barked in my face, then turned and glared at Darina, putting his ears back.

I hesitated. "Does he understand what we're saying?"

"No," Darina said. "He was never human. He was born a hound." The pup grinned at her, lolling his tongue out, and I felt briefly betrayed. Couldn't *anyone* prefer me? "He's cute, isn't he? I call him Leo."

I glared at her. We were not on a discussing-the-cuteness-of-puppies basis, and she knew it.

Grandma cleared her throat. Her face had gone grim

and focused, the way it did when the soup was about to boil over or she suspected the milkman had over-charged us.

Darina and I instinctively leaned slightly away from her. But before Grandma could speak, the door slammed open.

My father, of course, didn't bother to knock. He stalked straight into the kitchen as if he had a right to be there and said, "Well, *you*'ve created quite a ruckus."

It wasn't immediately clear which of us he meant by *you*, so we all stiffened. (Including Leo, who slid off my lap and hid under the table.) Darina spoke first. "What are you talking about?"

"A mob of very upset villagers is on their way here. I'm only a few minutes ahead of them."

A cold feeling slithered through my stomach. Sederic had told them about me. Of course he had. They knew, now, what I was, and they had come to—

"They want to send Darina back to the castle," my father said.

I blinked. "What?"

"They're saying that she escaped the Beast, and that it's only a matter of time before he comes here to hunt her down. Her, and anyone who stands in his way."

I remembered the Beast's huge jaws, his fierce eyes, the focused savagery in his voice: *I won't let you take her away.*

"That's not true," Darina said. "I didn't flee. He *let* me go! He knows I'm coming back."

My father gave her an exasperated look. *I* was used to those looks, but Darina was not, and her cheeks reddened. "And if he didn't know that?" my father said. "Would he let you go? If you wanted to be free?"

"I don't want to be free! I mean, I am free!"

"You didn't answer his question," I pointed out.

Darina glared at me.

"Regardless," my father snapped, "there's a mob practically at your door."

"Stop saying *mob*," I said. "It's just some villagers." I sounded like I was trying to convince myself. I tried to strengthen my voice. "They're probably bringing us meat pies."

"No," my father said. "They're not bringing meat pies."

"True," I conceded. "They didn't have time to bake any."

My father looked past me impatiently. Grandma met his gaze. Her mouth formed a thin line.

"It's only some villagers," I repeated. This time it came out sounding like a question. "They just want to know what's going on."

Grandma hesitated, then said, "Bolt the door."

I stared at her. "You're not serious!"

"It wouldn't make a particularly funny joke."

"But this is ridiculous," Darina said. "You can't think we're in danger from our neighbors!"

"Really?" Grandma said. "What do you think the villagers will do if they think you've made the Beast angry? If they think he'll take his wrath out on them?"

"But he wouldn't!"

"Yes, well. They don't know about his newly sweet nature." Before I had time to figure out if she was being sarcastic, Grandma marched over to the door. She lifted her hand, then dropped it and sighed. "How long has this bolt been broken?"

"Stop it!" Darina said. "This isn't necessary. No one wants to see me get hurt."

Which was true. Not that she had done anything to deserve it; she was just used to a certain baseline level of approval, which she got simply for being beautiful.

Grandma turned to her. "This village has been letting the Beast take people for years, one by one, rather than stand up to him. They let him kidnap you. Yes, yes"—she held up a hand—"I know it wasn't like that, you *wanted* to be imprisoned." Okay, she was definitely being sarcastic. "But they didn't know that, did they? They thought you were his prisoner, trapped in his castle, turned into one of his hounds, and they let it happen. So what makes you think they'll change now?"

"They will," she said.

There was no conviction in her voice, but that was only because she was no good at arguing. She really believed they would make an exception for her. Everyone had always treated her like she was special, and deep down, too deep for reason to matter, she believed it too.

Sure enough, the next thing out of her mouth was, "I'll just go out and explain everything."

Someone pounded on our front door, which immediately flew open.

We turned to face the mass of people on our doorstep. They were all familiar faces, but there was something about their expressions that was not quite so familiar. Or maybe it was just that they all had nearly the same expression, as if there was only one emotion among all of them.

The blacksmith stepped forward. He inclined his head to Grandma, who inclined hers back, and then he looked at Darina.

"So it's true," he said. "She's escaped the Beast."

The people behind him shifted. I saw the seamstress with her lips pressed together, her arms crossed over her chest, and the baker with her arm around her older daughter, holding her protectively close.

"I haven't escaped." Darina stepped into the center of the kitchen. "The Beast let me go."

The fishmonger looked skeptical. "Did he, now?"

"What have you done, Darina?" the woodcutter asked. His wife was with him, and they were holding hands tightly; she was trembling. "You've put us all in danger with this recklessness."

A murmur of agreement rose from behind him.

"No," Darina said. "You have it all wrong."

"Do we?" The fruit-seller stepped up. "If he thinks we're hiding you, he'll kill us all. My grandmother saw him in a rage once, and she tells the story to this day."

"We're sorry for your family," the butcher said apologetically—to Grandma, still not to Darina. No one was looking at her, which was ridiculous. People *always* looked at her. "It isn't right, what you've gone through. But it still isn't fair for the rest of us to suffer."

A voice from the back of the crowd: "For the good of the village, she has to go back to him. Now."

People glanced at each other. Some faces were uncomfortable, others . . . excited. I felt like a rabbit must right before it senses a predator: terrified of any motion that might trigger the hunter's urge to strike.

But no—that was just my father getting into my head. These were my friends. Well, they were Grandma's friends. Darina's friends. I had known these people all my life. I had imagined that if I rescued Darina, I could count on them for help.

Now I felt that all it would take was for one of them to step over the doorstep and the hunt would be on.

I looked through the crowd, desperate for a friendly face. I was hoping to see Sederic, but he wasn't there. Talya was standing near the back, glancing uncomfortably at the people around her.

"Mera!" Ressa pushed her way to the front of the crowd, shoving several people out of her way. I drew in a breath, my muscles quivering with tension, but she smiled at me. "Is it true what I've heard? That Darina is going to *marry* the Beast?"

A murmur ran through the crowd like a ripple, this time more confused than angry.

How did Ressa know that, when *I* had just learned it? Before I could start to wonder at that mystery, Darina ran to Ressa and threw her arms around her.

"Yes," she said. "It's true. We're going to be married!"

Silence.

Darina smiled, and I could almost see the effects of her smile rippling through the crowd. "The Beast has been under a curse for hundreds of years," she announced. "That curse has extended to our village. But we have, at last, found a way to break it. He will turn into a man, and we will be wed, and the castle will become a place of protection, not a place of fear."

How flowery and . . . nonsensical. She had definitely

spent too much time with Sederic. But the villagers were looking at each other, their whispers taking on a different tone, and I found myself suddenly able to breathe.

"That gown!" Ressa shrieked. "Darina, it's *amazing!*"

"How do we know you're telling the truth?" the baker demanded. "If this is just a ploy, if you're actually trying to escape him, who knows what he will do?"

"It is the truth," Darina declared. "I've just come for a short visit. I'm going back to the castle tomorrow morning."

I made a small sound of protest, but no one heard me.

"That's good news," the butcher said. "We'll come tomorrow morning to escort you."

My father cleared his throat. "There's no need for that."

He shouldn't have spoken. I knew it the second eyes turned on him.

"Easy for you to say," the miller snapped. "You're not one of us. You'll be gone on one of your ships by the time the Beast comes to take his vengeance."

My father's face paled, but he didn't back down. He opened his mouth, and I tried to think of a way to stop him from saying . . . whatever he was about to say. I had no idea what it was, but I was sure it would only make things worse.

"It's all right." Darina, apparently, had come to the same conclusion. She stepped in front of our father, the hem of her gown sweeping the floor. "I will be grateful for your escort. It will help me convince the Beast to invite you all to our wedding."

I could tell she was lying—though I wasn't sure about what—but everyone else seemed to believe her. In the silence, Ressa squealed with delight.

"Thank you for coming," Darina said. Her voice trembled the slightest bit, but I was probably the only one who noticed. "Please let me have this evening with my family."

"We'll see you at sunrise," the butcher said, and made an awkward sort of half bow. "Be ready to leave then."

He didn't say: *Whether you want to go or not.*

Then again, he didn't really have to.

16

Once the door had shut behind the villagers, Leo bounded out from under the table and raced to the doorway. He barked loudly and ferociously at the closed door, then looked at us over his shoulder to make sure we all noticed how bravely he was protecting us.

"I think they really would have dragged you back," I said. "I think that's why they came. To see if they would have to."

My voice came out smaller than I had thought it would. Grandma reached out and pulled me close, and I gave in to the urge to bury my face in her dress. It was soft and smelled like herbs.

"They're afraid," Grandma said. "Scared people turn on each other, and they're merciless toward anyone they've decided is a threat. Just like a pack of dogs or wolves would be."

I rolled my eyes, though with my face buried in her side, she couldn't see it. "I've only been part of a pack *once*, Grandma. You don't need to start making analogies to hounds all the time."

"I've only made an analogy to hounds once." She paused. "So far."

I laughed. She kept an arm around my shoulder as I straightened.

"They're right to be scared," my father said. "And don't think they won't turn on you if they're pushed to it. If we want to get you to safety, we have only tonight to do it."

"I *am* safe," Darina said. "The Beast won't let anyone hurt me. I don't need to go anywhere."

Our father looked at her, and something like pity flashed in his eyes. He opened his mouth as if to speak, then closed it, his shoulders sagging.

"I have to go," he said. "I need to check on my horse."

Grandma crossed her arms over her chest as she watched him leave.

"Darina," she said, and, much to my satisfaction, my sister flinched. "We need to talk." She turned to me. "Mera, go buy some eggs, some flour, and some beans."

My mouth dropped open. "You want me to go *shopping* right now?"

"I need to make dinner, don't I?" Grandma said. "I can't

have you just eating porridge. And it's for three people now. Probably four."

"I should be here when you talk to Darina," I protested. "I've learned a few things about the Beast and his castle that you might find relevant."

"I'm sure you have." She patted my shoulder. "But there are things I know, too. Things I need to discuss with Darina privately."

An old, familiar resentment flickered through me. Everyone loved Darina best—I was used to that, and didn't mind much. After all, not one of them loved her half as much as I did. But it still sometimes rankled that *Grandma* trusted Darina more than she did me.

It's like nothing has changed, I thought, and my jealousy immediately vanished. Because if only that were true. If we could go back to how things had been, I would gladly endure Grandma's preferences and Darina's insufferable saintliness and both of their constant promises to explain things when I was old enough.

Besides, maybe Grandma would be able to do what I hadn't, and make Darina see sense.

"All right," I said. I stomped to the door. "I'm leaving. But you had better hope no one asks me any questions, because I don't think you'll like the answers I'm going to give."

It had turned into a gray, foggy day, the sky a blurred white, the air threatening rain but not quite raining. It suited my mood perfectly. I closed the door so fast that Leo didn't get a chance to try to follow me, then hunched my shoulders as I walked to the market, trying to give off a don't-talk-to-me vibe.

Guess how well that worked.

Talya descended upon me as soon as I stepped foot in the village square. Clearly, she had been watching and waiting for someone to leave the house. She had probably been hoping for Darina, but she seemed willing to settle for me.

Which did not bode well. Talya had never before approached me voluntarily. Every muscle in my body tensed. If Sederic had told just one person the truth about me, it would be Ressa . . . but if Ressa knew, wouldn't I have seen some sign of it earlier? And if Ressa had told Talya, surely everyone would know by now.

"Why does your face look even more sour than usual?" Talya asked, falling into step beside me. "I thought you'd be happy Darina is back."

My relief was so vast that I forgot to ignore her. "I would be happy if she was back to stay. But she's not, thanks to all of you."

It had sounded biting in my head. It came out sullen and childish. Talya gave me a withering look. "You know that was never possible."

"We have no idea what's possible," I said, against my better judgment. "We've all been too afraid of the Beast to stand up to him."

"For good reason," Talya pointed out. "And Darina has no right to put the whole village in danger. Though if what she said is true, maybe it's a good thing the Beast took her."

Once again, I spoke against my better judgment. (Sometimes I wonder what the point is of my having better judgment to begin with.) "It's never a good thing to be kidnapped, Talya."

"It seems to have worked out well in the end. Darina looked happy. *And* well dressed."

"That's only because—and she doesn't even—" I spluttered and started walking again, faster than before. Talya rushed after me, her shoes clattering on the ground.

My palms hurt. When I looked down, I saw indentations deep in my skin. One of them was welling up slightly with blood, and my nails were longer and sharper than they should have been.

"Ressa thinks it's romantic," Talya went on, without

concealing her glee. "It's like Sederic said in that song! *A beauty so radiant that it affects even the most savage beast, there is no one as beautiful in the north or south or east...*"

I stopped walking and turned to face her. I had never physically attacked Talya—well, not since that time four years ago—but my fists were clenched at my sides, and the urge to hurt her was almost as strong as the urge to shift. I wasn't sure I could control both impulses at once.

Whatever Talya saw on my face, it actually—for a wonder—made her stop talking. She stepped back.

"Well," she said after a moment, with a flip of her hair, "the whole village is talking about nothing else. So you had better get used to acting like you're happy about it."

One of the worst things about Talya was that the more annoying she was, the more likely she was to be right.

First I was stopped by the candlemaker, asking if I knew that he needed a week's advance notice to create festive carved candles. ("Something to really make an event special...") Then by the winemaker, wanting me to let Darina know that he had several casks of wine available for her to sample. Then by the baker, insisting that I take an entire—freshly baked, by the smell of it—meat pie.

I took it. Grandma was right, after all: there were likely four of us who needed dinner that night—plus

Leo. And I was starting to suspect that I wouldn't be getting much shopping done.

Then Madam Nikkia, the seamstress, stopped me to let me know how difficult it was to get white fabric, and the cobbler urged me to stop in later to look at his new collection of fancy party shoes, and I passed a group of children practicing wedding dances in the town square. They were singing a song clearly written by Sederic: a mournful *"She is gone forever, I will forget her never,"* followed by the uplifting, if illogical, *"But my love will never die, no matter how many tears I cry."*

The tune was much better than the lyrics. It was so catchy that even *I* found myself humming *"The healing will start, deep down in my heart"* as I approached my house.

Where Sederic was waiting, dressed all in black, his face drawn and pale.

I stopped short. For a frantic moment, I wondered if I could run back down the street, go around the marketplace, and approach the house from the back ... but he was already looking at me. And anyhow, I had to find out who he had told about me. Or who he was planning to tell.

The meat pie was still hot from the oven, and it was burning my palm. I shifted it to my other hand as I approached him, trying to keep my chin up and my mouth firm. I wasn't sure what expression my face was making, except that I was pretty certain that if I could have seen it, I wouldn't have been happy with it.

"Mera," Sederic said, inclining his head.

Which was pretty stiffly formal, and not how he'd ever spoken to me in the past. But it was better than him turning around and running from me in horror. So I did my best to nod back.

"I'm sorry," he said.

I froze. "Why? Who did you tell?"

He looked confused, then seemed to mentally shrug and go on with his prepared speech. "I'm sorry that I left you behind at the castle. By the time I realized you hadn't followed me, I was lost among the trees."

"Oh," I said. "That's, um, that's all right." I took a deep breath. "Did you tell anyone what I . . . what you saw me do?"

"No," he said.

It took me a moment to hear it, and another moment to realize I believed him. "Why—why not?"

He gave me a puzzled look. "You asked me not to."

"But—" I remembered his trembling voice: *You're one of them.* "Aren't you . . . afraid of me?"

He looked at me as if the question was ridiculous. Which, honestly, was a little insulting.

"I know you would never hurt your sister," he said.

Darina's stricken face flashed in front of my eyes. "No.

I would not. And I am not beholden to the Beast like the other hounds are."

"I didn't think you would be," he said. "You're tougher than Darina is."

"Darina's tough," I protested.

He gave me a skeptical look, then shrugged. "I must see her, Mera."

I coughed. "I don't know if that's the best idea. You've heard what they're saying?"

"I have. But I don't believe she would marry that monster of her own free will. It doesn't make any sense."

"No," I agreed. "It doesn't."

"She's not herself. How could she be? She's been trapped in a place of darkness and shadows, of enchantment and dark mirrors." Which sounded like a line he was already planning for a song. I wondered what he was going to rhyme with *mirrors*. "She has been driven half out of her mind by all those terrors—"

Hmm. Not the best rhyme, but that didn't tend to bother Sederic.

"—forced to rely on the Beast for her protection. She got confused, and who wouldn't?"

"Well," I said, "I'm pretty sure I wouldn't."

"She can return to her true self. We can help her. All she needs is time with the people who truly care for her, away from the castle and the Beast."

Like the rhyme, that was probably close enough to the truth.

But Darina didn't have time. The villagers were going to bring her to the castle in the morning.

"Please," Sederic said. "Beg her to grant me the favor of a word."

I sighed. "If I say no, I suppose you'll pester us by throwing pebbles at her window and reciting poems outside our house all night?"

"I will do everything in my power to let her know she has my eternal devotion," Sederic said earnestly.

"Right." I rested the pie against my side. "I think she's talking to my grandmother now. Come tomorrow morning at dawn." I wasn't sure what good Sederic could do against a mob of villagers. Maybe he could talk sense into them. Or sing an inspiring song or something. "But if she doesn't want to see you—"

"I'll leave," Sederic promised. "And never darken your door again."

"I'm sure." I put one hand on the door in question. "Aren't you afraid, though? Even if Darina is all right with you declaring your eternal devotion, I can't imagine the Beast will like it much."

The tips of Sederic's ears turned red, but he lifted his chin. "My love gives me courage, and with courage I strengthen my love."

"Okay," I said.

I waited until Sederic walked away, his steps long and heavy. Then I opened the door.

Darina jumped, whirling to face me. She stepped sideways, but not quickly enough to hide that she had been crouching over Grandma's open medicine chest.

I stopped short in the doorway. "What are you doing?"

"I—um, I'm—" Darina swallowed. "Grandma went upstairs to rest, and I'm looking for willow bark. I have a headache."

I stared at her, then put the meat pie down on the entrance rug and stalked over to the medicine chest. Darina backed away.

I was very familiar with my grandmother's medicine chest. I helped her reorganize it at least once a month. The chest was divided into six compartments, mostly filled with glass bottles, tied-up pouches, bandages, or scissors and various other implements. Everything looked almost the same as usual.

But the bottle of rose powder was crooked. Grandma would never have put it back crooked.

I touched the bottle with one finger. Then I looked at Darina, who had two bright red spots of color high on her cheeks.

"You didn't miss us," I said. My insides felt hollow, and

my outsides felt numb. "And you didn't want to apologize to me. That's not why you came back."

"Mera..."

I stood, and she stopped talking. Something was gathering behind my numbness, something hot and sharp and painful, but for now my voice emerged clear and emotionless.

"You came back," I said, "to steal from us."

17

A small, ridiculous part of me expected Darina to deny it. But she didn't. She stood perfectly still, her chin trembling, avoiding my gaze.

Rage fizzed through me. If I had been in hound form, I would have leapt right for her throat.

I wished I *was* in hound form. Then rage would be all I was feeling.

"That's why the Beast told you to come home," I said. "He realized that we have a bottle of powder from his roses, and he decided he wants it." It was hard to talk, as if something many-barbed was taking up space in my chest. "So he sent you back to your family to rob us."

"He didn't send me!" Darina said. "He didn't even want me to leave. This was my idea."

I had thought I was angry before. That had been nothing compared to the fury that scorched through me now. "Really. You *wanted* to betray your family, to steal from Grandma—"

"It's his powder!" Darina said. "Our ancestors stole it from him first."

She folded her arms across her chest, as if she had made an irrefutable argument and now merely had to wait for me to agree with her.

I was worried that when I spoke, I would cry. To my relief, my voice came out sharp and bitter instead. "Gee, I wonder why. Maybe they thought that if they couldn't control the change, he would keep them trapped forever in his pack."

"That's *not* what he wants!" she shouted. "He's changed. He wants to be human. This powder could help him. And once he changes, it might set all the hounds free."

"Is that what he told you?" My fury was getting hotter by the second, and that was good. It felt better than anything else I could possibly be feeling. "And of course you believed him—"

"I *do* believe him!" Darina, unlike me, had no hesitation about crying. Normally the sight of her tears made me soften with guilt, no matter what we were fighting about, but now it only made me angrier. How dare she act like *she* was the one being hurt and disappointed? "I *know* him! Even if you can't let go of your prejudice against him, can't you trust me? Do you think I'm a fool?"

"Yes," I snapped. Darina looked like I'd struck her. "I mean—you've *been* fooled. He's kept you isolated for months, he's been wearing you down—"

"It wasn't like that!" She clenched and unclenched her fists. "He loves me!"

"Do you honestly believe that?" Even as I said it, I knew it was pointless. "You know he didn't keep you imprisoned in his castle because he was enraptured by your beauty. He did it because he thought you could get the rose powder for him!" I took a deep breath. "After Father tried to steal a rose from his castle, he realized that someone in our family knew what the roses were for. He didn't even want *you*, specifically. When he sent that message, he was hoping to get someone who could turn into a hound. He meant it for me."

She didn't react to that. Probably because, even with everything she knew, it made no sense to her that anyone would prefer me to her. It would make no sense to anyone, which was why I had never spoken of it. "I can't do this anymore, Mera. I feel like I've had this conversation with you a million times!"

"In that case," I snapped, "you'd think you'd be better at it by now."

"Don't you see? This is why I had to sneak into the

medicine chest, why I couldn't just talk to you and Grandma. You're so set against him that you won't listen!"

"He locked me in a cell! He almost killed me! Don't you *care?*"

"He didn't almost kill you," Darina said defensively. "If he wanted to kill you, you would already be dead."

"Oh, excellent point. You should definitely marry him, then."

Darina hugged her arms to her chest. "You saw how angry he was in the garden, but he stopped when I asked him to." Her voice softened. "He would never hurt me."

"Because he loves you?"

"Yes!"

"But if he didn't love you, he *would* hurt you. And you're all right with that?"

"That's not—he doesn't—it's complicated!"

"Things often are when they don't make sense!"

Darina pressed her lips together. "You're too young to understand."

That did it. I reached down and pulled the glass bottle out of the medicine chest. Then I whirled and stalked to the door.

"Where are you taking that?" Darina demanded.

"Nowhere." I yanked the door open. "I'll bring it back. I'm just making sure no one steals it while I'm out. Not that I can think of anyone who would do something so disgusting."

"Stop." Darina lunged forward and grabbed my arm. "Mera, please. Just let me take it—then he'll be human, and you'll see—"

"I don't care if he's human!" I yanked my arm away and whirled to face her. "He'll still be a kidnapper and a thief. He'll still be the monster who terrified our village for centuries." I hesitated, then lobbed out my most devastating weapon. "He'll still be the one who killed our mother."

Darina froze. "No, he didn't."

I had asked Grandma once whether the Hunt had killed our mother, whether that was why her body had been found in the forest. Grandma had responded without looking at me, but with a tone in her voice that let me know to never bring it up again: *Not exactly.*

Which wasn't a no.

"He had something to do with her death, and you know it! We've *always* known it! How can you—"

Darina lunged forward and grabbed the bottle out of my hand.

I should have expected it. If she had been anyone else, I would have.

I yelped and swiped for it, too late. She stepped back, holding it high over her head, out of my reach. Her lips were pressed together so tightly that they pulled deep creases along the sides of her mouth.

"I'm sorry," she said. "You left me no choice." She stepped around me, into the doorway.

I threw myself sideways at her.

She *had* been expecting that, and she dodged out of my way and sprinted outside. But she stepped on the hem of her long dress and stumbled, and in that moment, I grabbed her right arm. I yanked it downward and snatched the bottle back.

She pushed, I twisted, and suddenly the bottle went flying through the air. There was a thud and a crash, and the distinct tinkle of breaking glass.

And then, for a second, utter silence.

"No!" Darina scrambled to her feet and slid across the ground. "*No.*"

I closed my hand, disbelieving, around empty air.

Darina was on her knees, trying to scrape rose powder from the ground with her fingers. She yelped and drew her hand back, blood welling up where one of the glass shards of the bottle had cut her. "What have you done?"

"What have *I* done?" I repeated. "This was *your* fault!"

"You've ruined everything." She got to her feet, shaking all over. "If you think this will keep me away from the Beast, you're wrong. Even if he's cursed to be trapped forever, even if I can never marry him, I still won't leave him all alone. And I don't care if I never see *you* again."

"Make sure you tell the Beast that," I retorted. "Maybe it will keep him from forcing me to be a hound this time."

Her face twisted. For a moment, she actually looked ugly. She turned her back on me and stalked down the path, in the direction of the castle and the Beast.

"Oh, sure!" I shouted after her. "Leave it to me to clean up this mess!"

"You're the one who made it," she snapped over her shoulder. "And you can be the one to explain to Grandma—"

"Mera? Why are you shouting?" Our grandmother's thin voice floated through the air. "Darina? Where are you going?"

Darina froze. She turned and looked up at the window where my grandmother stood. I moved instinctively to block Grandma's view of the broken glass.

"Are you leaving again?" Grandma said. "Without telling me?" She put both hands on the windowsill and leaned out. Her long white braid fell over her shoulders, wisps escaping and fluttering across her face. "What are the two of you yelling about?"

Darina looked at me, and every muscle in my body tensed. No matter how angry we were, how bitter our fights, we never told on each other. Never. She had covered for me, and I had covered for her, so many times. About sneaking out at night, about taking the last fruit tart, about breaking Grandma's vase, about . . . about everything.

Including, apparently, about my turning into a hound. Darina had known, and she had never breathed a word.

But none of our fights had been as bad as this.

"Nothing," Darina said. "Just a . . ." She spent a few seconds trying to come up with a word, then gave up. "I'm not leaving. Not yet."

"Then come back inside," Grandma's voice grew fainter as she moved away from the window. "It's time to have dinner. Mera, how did the shopping go?"

———◆———

Dinner was tense. Darina sat silent, radiating fury, and I was no better. I knew I had to tell Grandma that the powder was gone, but she was clearly still tired; she kept closing her eyes, and at one point she snored for a few seconds before shaking herself awake. She didn't miss anything, since neither Darina nor I said a word to each other the entire meal.

I surprised myself by eating heartily—the knot in my stomach was not tight enough to block how hungry I was. Plus, the meat pie was delicious. Leo positioned himself under my chair, looking at me with big hopeful eyes, and gobbled up every piece I slipped to him. There was plenty to go around, since my father never showed up.

Grandma went upstairs as soon as dinner was done. Her snores rumbled through the kitchen a few minutes later.

Darina frowned at the stairs. "She gets tired more easily now, doesn't she?"

"Well." I started stacking the plates to bring to the washbasin. "The past months have been difficult for her."

Darina's cheeks went pink. But she just lowered her head and started gathering the cups.

Words crowded my mind, fighting to get out. But I clamped my lips shut. What was the point? It was obvious that nothing I said could get through Darina's romance-addled head.

I wouldn't give up on her. Never. But arguing with her over and over *was* giving up. Because it was never going to work.

Not giving up on her didn't mean fighting with her. It meant finding another way.

And I was starting to have an inkling of what that other way might be.

I didn't look at Darina again as I walked past her, up

the stairs toward my room. I left the stacked plates on the table. She could clear and wash up by herself.

It seemed like the very least she could do.

———◆———

I had no intention of talking to Darina that night, so I got right into bed. Or tried to. There was something large and furry sprawled over the mattress, and when I yanked at my blanket, it growled at me.

It was Leo. Who wasn't that large, but had somehow managed to stretch his legs and head out so that he covered the mattress from one end to the other.

"Hey!" I said. "Get back to the kitchen. If you get fur on the blanket, Grandma will kick you out of the house."

Leo put one paw over his muzzle and went back to sleep.

He was right not to be worried; Grandma wouldn't really put him out. She would make *me* clean the blanket, though.

"Come on," I said. I took the section of blanket he was on and pulled it, spilling him onto the mattress in a gangly tumble of paws and tail.

He got to his feet, yipped at me, and grabbed the edge of the blanket between his teeth. He dragged it back across the mattress and sprawled on top of it.

I put my hands on my hips. Then I heard a creak on the stairs.

Darina.

The panic that rushed through me was completely out of proportion. It wasn't as if she was coming to attack me. But I didn't want to look at her, and I didn't want to talk to her. I needed to be in bed, with my eyes closed and my back to her, before she came into the room.

I shoved Leo hard. He didn't budge.

I didn't have time to wrestle him off my bed. (Nor was I sure I could.) So I scrambled onto the one thin edge of bed that didn't have dog on it and lay straight as a stick, balancing precariously and trying to look like I was asleep.

Leo put his head on top of my stomach. He began to snore just as Darina's form appeared in the doorway.

I closed my eyes and made my breathing deep and even. Darina's footsteps stopped halfway across the room. There was something heavy about the silence. I was sure she was standing near my bed, looking at me.

I resisted the temptation to open my eyes and peek. Finally, she moved again, past my bed to her own.

It took her, as usual, a torturously long time to get into bed. Apparently, being engaged to a monster didn't mean you didn't brush your hair a hundred times or slather your face and hands with half a dozen fancy

creams. (Darina had *lots* of creams; every time our father came to visit, he brought her more.) But finally she
settled into bed, and shortly after that her snores began
their familiar rhythm.

Cautiously, I opened my eyes. Darina's unthinkably
expensive gown was crumpled over the foot of her bed,
and her satin shoes lay on the floor, one next to the bed,
the other halfway between her bed and mine. Grandma
would have something to say about that tomorrow
morning—

I caught myself. By tomorrow morning, Grandma
might have other things to think about.

I sat up and pulled my boots back on, and then it was
my turn to stand over my sister's bed and watch her.
She looked so peaceful and innocent, with her eyelashes
throwing shadows on her cheeks and her shiny hair
spread across her pillow. I thought about putting a hand
on her shoulder, shaking her awake, sitting down to talk.

Just a day ago, I would have said I knew my sister better than I knew anyone else in the world. But now I felt
like I was looking at a stranger.

A day ago, I would never have imagined what she was
capable of, or how quickly she could turn on her family.

A pure, cold determination filled me. The truth,
which I could see now, was that I never *had* known her.
Not really. I'd built up a vision of her in my mind: a

strong, loyal protector. It was what I'd needed her to be after my mother died and my father all but vanished. And Darina had tried to be what I needed. She had a tendency to be what people wanted her to be.

I just wasn't the person whose wants she cared about. Not anymore.

There was nothing to be gained by talking to her. I would never get her to agree with me. I would never convince her to leave the Beast.

But that didn't mean I couldn't save her.

I knew now what I had to do in order to set my sister free.

Whether she liked it or not.

18

I crept down the stairs and spent several minutes getting out the front door, opening and closing it with excruciating slowness to keep it from squeaking. Once I was finally outside, I took a deep breath of chill night air. The sky was a murky black, clouds roiling under the blurred moon, and the trees' bare, gnarled branches looked dark and wrathful.

I started down the moonlit street, my boots thudding softly against the ground. It wasn't quite as late as I'd thought. Even though most of the homes were dark, I could see light flickering through the occasional window.

That was good. It meant my father would probably still be awake.

Something yowled and I stopped short. A moment later, the baker's cat streaked across the street in front of me and straight up a tree, where it hissed from the branches. I frowned, wondering what had gotten it so upset, then kept walking.

I almost stumbled over something small and heavy in the street in front of me. The thing yelped. I staggered but remained upright, and Leo leapt straight up into the air in front of me, his tail wagging energetically. He began racing around in front of me in tiny frantic circles.

"Stop. You're making me dizzy." But I couldn't help grinning. "You want to come with me?"

He leapt up again, all four feet in the air.

"Fine." It wasn't like I had much choice. And the truth was, I was glad he was there. "Just be quiet."

He responded with a series of extremely loud barks.

I started walking again. Leo dashed in front of me, looked over his shoulder, dashed back, wagged his tail encouragingly, and ran forward again. He continued doing that all the way to the inn.

Well, it was nice that *someone* was enthusiastic. It made me feel a little bit less like I was walking to my own execution.

It also made me jealous. I could, if I wanted to, be a pup just like him. We could romp around the village together, with nothing on our minds but all the exciting scents and delicious food and enormous fun the world offered. The weight pressing down on me would vanish, just like that.

But I knew now that the temptation running through me was a trap. It made me feel like shifting would be an escape, would turn me into something wild and free. But all it would really do was make me part of the Beast's pack, subject to his rule. The freedom I'd yearned for all my life was a lie. Just like the love Darina thought *she* was feeling.

Unlike her, I had seen the trap before I fell into it.

The village's inn and tavern was at the bottom of a fairly steep hill, far enough from town that the noise didn't bother us, close enough that my father often ate there even when he slept at our house. It had only a handful of rooms, because we didn't get that many travelers, but the tavern on the ground floor was popular with local villagers. The few times I had been sent there to retrieve my father, or to give Ressa a message from Darina, it had been full of people.

At this hour it wasn't full at all. There were a couple of men from the village sitting around a table playing cards, two women having an intense conversation that involved a lot of arm-waving, and a trader I didn't recognize eating stew in the corner. The innkeeper was nowhere to be seen, but Talya and Ressa were wiping down tables. Ressa seemed to be doing most of the work, and Talya was doing most of the complaining. Ressa looked up when I entered, shoving strands of black hair out of her face.

"Are you here to see Talya?" she asked.

"No," I said emphatically, but it was too late. Talya spotted me and glanced around the room, as if hoping Ressa might have been talking to someone else.

"I'm here to see my father," I said.

Ressa's eyes brightened and she leaned forward. Poised like a hunter, but her prey was gossip.

I braced myself for a barrage of questions, but suddenly Leo leapt into her arms, his tail a wagging blur. Ressa caught him and staggered back, and he swiped his tongue up her face.

"Leo!" I said. "What are you doing? Sorry, Ressa."

Ressa laughed, holding Leo in her arms as he wriggled with glee. "Friendly guy. Is he yours?"

"No," I said. "I guess not. He just likes everyone. Leo, get down."

At that moment, a man squeezed past us to go outdoors. Leo went still, put his ears back, and growled.

"Or . . . not everyone." I frowned at the man's back, but he was just the trader I hadn't recognized, and he hadn't so much as glanced at us. "He just likes you, I guess. Does he know you from somewhere?"

For some reason, Ressa looked guilty. "I've seen him around the inn, and I give him scraps. I've been calling him Sirius, but Leo suits him better." She tried to put Leo down, but he was having none of it; he twisted, grabbing her shoulders with his paws.

"Sorry," I said. "He's, um . . . not really trained."

"Sirius, sit!" Ressa said firmly.

Leo settled immediately on the floor, his tail thumping it with such force that it raised tiny clouds of dust.

Ressa wiped her face with her sleeve. "Make sure he doesn't try to steal anyone's food, all right? And take a seat." She shook out the rag, raining crumbs on the floor and on Leo. "At one of the tables we *haven't* cleaned yet, please."

I couldn't actually tell the difference; Ressa and Talya weren't that great at cleaning. But when I sat at a small table in the corner, as far from the other customers as I could get, Ressa didn't object. So I guessed it was an uncleaned one.

Leo looked curiously at the food on the other tables, his nose twitching. But to my relief, he jumped onto my lap, curled up, and went to sleep.

A few minutes later, my father walked into the tavern through the back door. Ressa said something to him, and he looked across the room at me. His eyes widened in surprise and he started over.

I braced myself. In my lap, Leo stirred and grumbled.

But all my father said, as he sat in the chair across from me, was, "Should you be here by yourself?"

"I'm not by myself," I said.

"I meant—"

"I know what you meant." No matter how ready I was for a fight, I couldn't afford to have one. Not with the last person who might be willing to help me. "Grandma won't be happy that I'm here. But she doesn't know where I am. Yet."

My father reached across the table and covered my hand with his. "Don't worry, Mera. She'll forgive you. She loves you too much not to."

For being in the tavern? Definitely.

For what I planned to do next? That, I wasn't so sure about.

I pulled my hand back into my lap and looked my father in the eye. The hair around his chin was gray, something I hadn't noticed until just now.

"Why did you go to the Beast's castle?" I asked.

His brow furrowed. "What?"

"I know you went to steal the last rose. But why did you want it? Was it really just because it would make you rich?"

His mouth twisted. "I suppose that wasn't all that believable."

Which wasn't entirely true. I had believed it the first time I heard it. But that was before I had seen the words he scratched in his prison cell, had watched him stand up to a mob in Darina's defense. It was possible that I had let my anger at my father cloud my judgment.

I didn't see any point in getting into any of that now. So I said, with as much self-assurance as I could muster, "No. Not really. But why didn't you tell me the real reason?"

Ressa came over and put a mug in front of my father. He took a long drink, waited until she walked reluctantly away, then said, "I didn't want to tell you because I didn't want you to feel guilty. You see, I went for the same reason you did."

My heart thumped. "I went to save Darina."

"Right." He put the jug down. "And I went to save you."

At the table in the corner, dice clinked.

I swallowed. "How did you find out—"

"I was coming back from the tavern, and I took a detour through the woods." My father turned the mug around in his hands. "I . . . saw you."

He didn't have to say what he had seen me doing. The disgust in his voice made it perfectly clear.

"You didn't see me. Or"—his face tightened—"smell me. I was downwind from you, and you were gone fast. So fast." He contemplated his mug, then lifted it and took another long swallow. "I might have thought it was my mind playing tricks on me—I'd had a bit too much to drink—but all at once, everything made sense. Things your grandmother had said, your mother's—" He broke off and downed the rest of the mug.

He seemed well on his way to having too much to drink *again*, and that would not be helpful. I cleared my throat. "Why did you think going to the Beast's castle would help?"

"Your mother once told me that the Beast had a rose, and that its petals could make him—or those like him—human. I never put together what she meant by *those like him* until I saw you. Even when she—" He looked down at his empty mug.

I reached across the table and pulled the mug away from him. "You thought you could steal the Beast's rose and use it to keep me human?"

"Yes." He laughed shortly. "I realize how ridiculous it sounds. I was scared of losing you, and I wasn't thinking clearly. It went about as well as you might expect."

"I saw the cell he put you in," I said.

"Yes. I was there for . . ." His voice drifted off. Something dark crossed his features, and he shook his head. "For a long time."

Fury made my chest so tight I couldn't speak. How

could Darina forgive the Beast for doing this to our father?

And how could I forgive *myself* for being the reason it had all happened?

"I failed you," he said. "I failed you both. I should have tried harder to figure out what was wrong with this village, and what it might turn you into."

His voice twisted with disgust, and my stomach curdled in response.

"I always suspected there was something different about the people here." He reconsidered. "Well, not *always*. But I knew there was something I didn't know. Your mother lied to me, and I could tell. But I didn't know what she was hiding."

"Why did you move here, then?" I demanded. "Why did you marry her?"

"Because I loved her, Mera. I loved her very much." My father ran a hand through his hair. "Enough to come live here in the back of nowhere, to accept all her silences and secrets. I thought they made her mysterious and alluring." He gave a choked laugh. "I was young and a fool. I didn't know what I know now: that love is precious and joyful, but in the end, it's a *feeling*. And feelings can change. By the time your mother died, her secrets had become a hedge of thorns between us. I was spending more and more time away, and . . ." His voice trailed off.

"And you weren't here when she died," I finished.

"I suppose your grandmother made quite a point of telling you that."

Grandma had never mentioned it. Only Darina had. But this didn't seem like the right time to point that out.

"I'll regret that forever. But I also know it wouldn't have made a difference if I had been here. She was pulling away from me by then, giving in to the lure of the pack. She cared more about them than she did about us." He sat back in his chair. "I should have accepted what was happening sooner. I should have taken you both away with me. I'm sorry that I didn't."

I dug my fingernails into my knees. My stomach was still tied up in a knot, and the tone of his voice made it pull tighter. But my voice emerged surprisingly steady.

"It's not too late," I said.

At least, I hope it's not.

He blinked at me. "To do what?"

"To take Darina away from here."

"She's made her choice, Mera. She's been quite clear on that."

"But she's *not* making a choice," I said. "The Beast made her think she is, but he's controlling her. It's magic. She wouldn't want to marry him otherwise."

My father lifted his eyebrows. "You think he put a love spell on her? That's ridiculous."

Which was an interesting word, coming from a man whose daughter could turn into a hound. "No, of course not. Not a spell, exactly. It's more . . . when you're part of a pack, you obey your pack leader. Darina's not . . . like me . . . but she's also descended from the original pack. Everyone in this village is. That's why none of us ever leave. Hounds don't leave their packs. They just don't."

"Then how do we take her away from him?" he demanded. "She won't listen to any of us."

"No," I agreed. "She won't." Which meant there was only one choice left. "We're going to do what the Beast did. Since apparently she finds it a perfectly acceptable method of changing people's minds."

His eyes narrowed. "You mean . . ."

I leaned over the table. "We're going to kidnap her back."

19

I braced my feet against the table legs, tensed for my father's reaction. But all he did was blink.

After several long seconds, I still couldn't tell what he was thinking, but his gaze was beginning to make me uncomfortable. I looked away. Ressa was cleaning the table right next to us, getting on her knees to scrub its underside, which I strongly suspected had not been cleaned since the day the table was made. But I was also pretty sure her blatant attempt to eavesdrop was not succeeding. We had kept our voices low, and there was no way she would still be scrubbing if she'd heard what I had just said.

My father cleared his throat. "All right," he said. "Let's do that, then."

In that moment, I forgave my father for everything: all those years he had stayed away, all that time that he hadn't been there for me. Because now, when it counted, he was going to help me.

I couldn't have said any of that, even if I wanted to. I tried to swallow the lump lodged in my throat, tried again, then just spoke around it. "I don't exactly have a plan yet."

"It's simple," my father said. "I was getting ready to ride to the port cities, to find out if any of my ships have come in. I can leave tonight, and I'll take the two of you with me. We'll sail to the Green Islands or one of the Sarial princedoms." His lips thinned. "I doubt the Beast can follow her across the ocean."

"He doesn't strike me as the type to let things go," I said. "When we come back—"

"We won't come back," my father said, as if that should have been obvious.

At the far table, dice clicked on wood, and a man swore. Ressa looked at us over her shoulder, but one of the customers called for more bread, and she left her washcloth on the table and went to the kitchen.

I tried to shove my feelings aside. My insides were a tangled mess of hope and hurt and fear, but none of it mattered.

"What about Grandma?" I asked.

"She'll never leave the village," my father said. "You know that."

I did know that.

"We'll send her a message to let her know you're both safe."

She would still be alone. But if we didn't do this, if the Beast took us both, she would be alone anyhow. At least this way she would know we were all right.

"Mera?" my father said.

I pushed my chair back. "We should go now," I said. "Darina's asleep. I mean, she was asleep when I left, and she's a deep sleeper."

My father shook his head. "We can't rely on a natural sleep. It will be at least next sunset before we reach a port city, especially with a loaded cart. She'll wake up, and I won't be able to stop her from running right back to him."

"What are you planning to do, then?" I asked. "Knock her unconscious?"

"I'll hardly have to *knock* her unconscious," my father said. "Your grandmother has a very potent sleeping dust in that medicine chest of hers. By the time Darina wakes up, she'll be on a ship, sailing farther from the Beast's influence with every passing day."

I imagined Darina wrapped in a blanket, her eyes tightly shut. Imagined her opening them to find herself in a ship's cabin, everything she had ever known slipping farther and farther away. Our village, our grandmother, the Beast.

I imagined Grandma waking up to find us both gone. I bit my lip. "Darina will be furious."

"I'm sure she will be."

It had never bothered my father when I was angry at him, either. "Not just furious. She'll hate us."

My father lifted his shoulders. "It's like you said. She forgave the Beast for kidnapping her. I'm sure she'll forgive us eventually, too."

I could hardly argue with that.

◆

We entered the house quietly, but we needn't have bothered; no one could possibly have heard us over the sound of Grandma's snoring. It filled the first floor, a series of almost rhythmic rumbles punctuated by regular, thunderous snorts. Leo flinched visibly and looked up at me reproachfully. Then he plodded over to the fireplace and curled up in front of it. After less than a second, his snores mingled with Grandma's.

My father went to the medicine chest, opened it, and rummaged for a moment before pulling out a small sack tied with a blue ribbon. I bristled. Grandma didn't let anyone touch her medicine chest without explicit permission, accompanied by exact instructions that she repeated at minimum five times.

"This is the sleeping dust," my father explained. He untied the pouch, sniffed it, then quickly tied it up again. "She used to give it to Li—to your mother when she had trouble sleeping. Even when she was pregnant. It's perfectly safe."

I wiped my sweaty hands on the sides of my skirt. "Right."

Lisara. I hadn't heard my mother's name in a long time. Grandma never talked about her. Darina did, sometimes, but never for long. It made her sad that I didn't remember my mother and didn't miss her. She was just gone—unlike Father, who showed up at random and unpredictable intervals, as if to emphasize the fact that most of the time he chose to stay away from us.

My father was still looking through the medicine chest. He lifted a bloodletting blade and turned it curiously from side to side.

"Put that down," I said. He blinked at me, and I realized how sharply I had spoken. I dug my nails into my arms, hugging them to my chest. "Let's just do this before I change my mind."

I had almost changed my mind a dozen times already. When we walked out of the tavern and Ressa gave me a sharp look. When we paid the grumpy stable boy and hitched my father's horse to his four-wheeled open cart. A cart that he normally used to transport goods, not people.

That was when I had come closest to telling my father that we should forget the whole thing. I had looked up at the Beast's castle, towers black against the sky, and then again at the cart. It had raised sides that should keep Darina safe enough, and the night was clear and not too cold. She would be wrapped in blankets . . . and she had never minded the cold anyway . . .

I'd reconsidered again when we led the horse up the road to the back of our house, and again when we snuck inside. But this was the first time I had mentioned my doubts out loud.

My father's eyes narrowed, and I immediately wished I had continued keeping my thoughts to myself. "I understand that this is difficult, Mera. But it's what's best for her. You know that."

He sounded so sure of himself. I had known he would be; that was part of why I'd gone to him with my plan in the first place. (Well, that, and the fact that he was the only person left I could go to.)

My father put the blade back in the chest. Crookedly. My fingers itched to straighten it. "Don't worry. Someday she'll thank you."

I doubted that. But I focused on the *you*. Did my father

think his job was just to get us on the ship, and then we would make our way in the world on our own?

Of course he did. Of course he would think that.

"We'll both have to take care of her," I said. "Until the Beast's hold on her is broken, someone will have to watch her all the time. And even after that . . . neither of us has ever been outside this village. We're going to . . ." I had to force the words out. "We're going to need you."

My father's lips quirked up slightly, the way Darina's did when she felt hurt. "Of course I'm going to take care of you."

"Okay," I said. "Well, good."

"Did you really doubt it?"

I assumed that was a rhetorical question.

"I know I haven't always been there for the two of you. But that was because your grandmother was raising you, and she made it clear she didn't need my help. Nor did she welcome my presence. I wasn't needed or wanted, but I still came, even though this village is a long way from my trade routes."

He sounded like he expected a medal.

I closed my eyes briefly. I had been angry at my father for so long that it had subsided into a banked, resentful simmer, nothing like my raging fury at Darina's betrayal. I didn't expect better from him. Or so I'd told myself.

But I was expecting better from him now. And if he

came through, if he upended his life to save us, did that mean I had been wrong about him all this time?

"Well," I said, "having me and Darina around will *also* interfere with your trade."

He sucked in his breath, and I thought of all those angry dinners, all those long, empty winter days when he'd said he would come and never showed up. I'd wished then that I had the power to hurt him. Now, somehow, I had it. And I didn't like it at all.

"It wasn't my business that kept me away." My father rubbed his eyebrows. "It was the secrets you all shared and kept from me. I should have fought harder for you, I know that. I offered to take you with me, many times. Both of you. Your grandmother wouldn't hear of it. She said you belonged in the village."

Those offers must have been made a long time ago, when we hadn't been old enough for him to make them directly to *us*. But I was inclined to resent my grand-mother at the moment, to start building my defenses againt my guilt about what we were doing to her. So I said, "She should have let us decide."

"I agree." My father's eyes narrowed. "But I always thought that if I asked, you would say no."

"I would have," I admitted. I had never wanted to live anywhere but this village. Despite the threat of the Beast, despite the Wild Hunt—or maybe because of those things—it was my home. It had never occurred to me to think about leaving. "But now I don't have a choice."

"Why don't you—" He stopped. "The Beast is after you, too?"

"Yes. Obviously. Now that he knows I can . . ." I gestured vaguely, not wanting to say it. "He thinks I belong in his pack."

My father's eyebrows drew together. "Why didn't you tell me that you were also in danger?"

"Because Darina's danger is more im—immediate."

He blinked at me. I wondered if he could tell that I had almost said *important*.

"Well," he said. "All the more reason to move swiftly, then." He started to shut the medicine chest, then glanced over at me. "Maybe we should bring some extra sleeping dust along for you. In small doses, it helps with snoring."

"What?" I said. "*I* don't snore!"

My father laughed. "You snore louder than your grandmother and your sister put together."

"That's not true."

"Have it your way." My father shrugged and closed the lid. "I'll bring Darina down. You make sure no one sees us carrying her out."

He started up the steps. I watched him go, my stomach

churning. I hadn't thought this through—my father drugging Darina, carrying her downstairs—

Maybe this was a mistake.

I turned and hurried across the kitchen, past Leo's slumbering form. I opened the front door just far enough to make sure the coast was clear.

"Mera!" Sederic cried. "I was just trying to decide whether I should knock."

The coast was not clear.

20

"I must see Darina now," Sederic declared. He was dressed completely in black—except for his boots, which were dark brown, probably because he owned only one pair of boots. Even the hollows under his eyes were sort of blackish-purple. "I know it's not yet sunrise, but I cannot hold myself back any longer."

"You were trying to hold yourself back until now?" I spoke as loudly as I could so my father would hear me and know not to come down with Darina.

"I would never stand in the way of her happiness. But I need to look into the depths of her eyes one last time and tell her what is in my heart."

I heard the stairs creak. I didn't dare look back, but I spoke even louder. "Everyone knows what's in your heart, Sederic. You've told her dozens of times! Most recently with that song at the midsummer ball—"

"Why are you shouting?"

"How did the lyrics go again? Oh, yes, I remember." I belted them out at the top of my lungs. *"I can't sleep for all my dreams of you, I can't eat while my heart screeeaaaammms for you—"*

"Not *screams*," Sederic corrected me, looking affronted. "It's *while my heart teems with love for you.*"

His voice (much nicer than mine) soared through the air.

"Oh, right, sorry. That *is* much better." I risked a glance over my shoulder. The stairs were still empty, and the only sound was my grandmother's and Leo's snores. I took a breath of relief.

Then I heard another creak.

Seriously?

"There is something you must know," I said to Sederic quickly, "before you, um, dump your heart—"

"*Unburden* my heart."

"Right. Before you do that. Let's talk outside."

He hesitated. I added as I ducked past him, "She told me this in private, but I think you have a right to know."

That worked. He followed me outside, and the door shut behind me. Now all I needed was for my father to pay a tiny bit of attention to what was going on around him.

"What did she tell you?" Sederic asked, and the pleading note in his voice sent a sharp stab of guilt through me. What would *he* think when he discovered what I had done to my sister?

Behind me, in the house, I heard heavy footsteps. *Seriously, Father?* I braced myself against the door, not sure what exactly I was planning to do—hold it shut against my father's weight? I wouldn't stand a chance. I tried to think of an excuse to get Sederic away from here, fast. "I, um, maybe we should go to . . . um . . ." There was nowhere in the village to go *to*, except the tavern, and there was no way Sederic was going to take me there. I covered my face with my hands to give myself time to think.

"There, there," Sederic said. "It's all right."

Nothing was all right. It turned out I wasn't pretending. My vision was blurred with tears.

I looked at Sederic through my fingers, and the pain on his face was an echo of how I felt. New guilt piled up on top of all the other guilt I was already feeling. All my life I'd treated Sederic with disdain—because, honestly, he made it easy to. But he truly loved Darina. He didn't really know her, but so what? Turned out, I hadn't known her that well, either.

I dropped my hands. Sederic deserved to know the truth.

"She's determined to marry the Beast," I said. "She won't listen to anyone—not me, and definitely not you. There's no point in trying. I'm sorry."

Sederic hunched his shoulders. I looked away from his stricken expression.

"I always thought she would leave this village," he said. "She used to talk about how she wanted to travel...."

I blinked. "She did?"

"Yes. She would only have done it once you were older, of course. She would never abandon you."

"Well," I said, "maybe not *never*."

"She dreamed that the two of you might go together. She wanted to see more places—to be admired by more people—to find out what the rest of the world had to offer. That was why I started training to be a minstrel— because minstrels travel. I thought she might want to come with me...." His voice broke. "But now she'll never leave. She'll be stuck here forever, just in a castle instead of a house. Is *that* what she really wanted, all this time? Should I have gone into trade instead?"

"No," I said. "Deep down, she still wants what she always wanted. She just ... forgot." I glanced involuntarily at the castle. "But it might not be too late. I think she might ... she might still get to see the world."

"I hope you're right," Sederic said. He hesitated. "Tell her I said so."

I watched him walk away, not moving until he disappeared around the bend in the street.

"I will," I said, too quietly for anyone to hear.

Then I turned and went back into the house.

———◆———

My father was sitting at the kitchen table, his shoulders hunched, in almost the exact same position he'd been in when I first saw him the night before. Except this time, of course, my grandmother wasn't with him.

And neither was Darina.

"Father?" I said. Maybe *he* had changed his mind. Maybe he'd been having the same doubts I had. In which case, it was a good thing that *I* was now certain, because it was my turn to convince him. We cared about Darina. We were doing what was best for her. It was either us kidnapping her or the Beast kidnapping her, and we were clearly the better choice. The fact that we had doubts *proved* that we were doing the right thing.

It was a great argument. But I never got a chance to use it. As I approached the table, my father lifted his head and said, "She's gone."

I stopped walking. "What?"

"Her bed was empty. She must have gone back to the Beast while we were at the tavern."

I drew in a breath. Darina *had* been lying earlier, just like I thought; she didn't want the villagers dragging her back to the castle. So she had gone on her own, before they could provide their "escort."

I wondered—a bit late—whether anyone from the village had been watching our house. But of course, they would have had no reason to stop her. Not when she was going exactly where they wanted her to go.

My father held up one hand. "She left this on her pillow, along with a note."

I walked over to get a good look at it. The white-gold ring with a flower-shaped quartz stone lay in his palm.

"It's your mother's ring," he said. "I gave it to her when we first got married. She never took it off. Or so I thought."

"But—but Darina said the Beast gave her that ring."

His jaw clenched. He turned the ring over in his fingers. "So Lisara was in the castle, and the Beast took it from her. I always knew he had something to do with her death." He closed his fist around the ring. "He's taken so much from us. But the two of us, we're going to get away from him now. We'll start over—"

"What? No!" I exclaimed. "We're not leaving without Darina."

He looked at me with deep pity, then lifted his other

hand, which had been flat on the table. Beneath it was a note, a small white paper with three short sentences in Darina's delicate, curlicued handwriting:

I have to go. I love him. Please don't hate me.

The *me* was smudged by what looked like a teardrop.

"She's gone, Mera," my father said. "We're too late."

"No. No, we're not." My heartbeat was so loud in my ears that I could barely hear my own voice. "We can go to the castle, we can still—"

The look on his face stopped me cold. He put the ring down on the table. "I'm not going back to that castle, Mera. Not ever."

"I don't want to, either," I said. Which was pretty much the definition of an understatement. "But if that's where Darina is—"

He held up one hand to stop me. "It's over, Mera. She left the ring for me because she knows who it belonged to, and then she went back to him. There's nothing more we can do."

"That's not true."

"No?" He laughed, a tired, bitter sound. "What would you suggest?"

"We go to the castle, and we—we talk to her. We explain . . ." He was about to laugh again, I could tell. My thoughts zigzagged frantically. "We'll bargain with the Beast."

His laugh burst out of him with a force that made me flinch. "Bargain with the *Beast?*"

"If that's what it takes, yes."

"And what exactly do we have to bargain with?"

"I have something he wants. Or, I mean, I know how to get something he wants. Maybe. Probably." Sensing that I was losing momentum, I went on quickly. "He wants the last rose, and he thinks I can find it for him. I'll tell him I'll do it as long as he sends Darina away."

I hadn't realized my father was actually listening expectantly until I saw the hope on his face die. "He won't do that, Mera."

"It's the reason he wanted her! The reason he was interested in our family to begin with. He realized that *you* knew something about the rose, and he was just hoping Darina would tell him what you would not."

"Maybe at first." My father shook his head. "But I saw them together before I left. I think his priorities have changed."

I stared. "You think he really loves her? That's ridiculous."

"Love is complicated, Mera. The Beast loves Darina, but he's still a monster. And I can't . . . I can't watch someone else I love throw her life away in that castle."

"You won't have to," I said. "We can still get her back."

"Believe me, Mera, I'd risk everything to save her. But

I can't. I can only save you." He got heavily to his feet, leaving the ring on the table. "And I'd rather do that than lose you both."

I shook my head.

"Mera." His voice was very quiet. "I'm doing this for you. You're my daughter as much as Darina is. If I haven't seemed to pay as much attention to you, it's only because I didn't think you needed as much. You were always stronger than her." He managed a half smile. "I suppose you had to be."

He didn't seem to realize that was an insult.

When I was younger, I hadn't known I wasn't pretty. I'd thought the difference between me and Darina was that she was soft and gentle and sweet, and I was fierce and prickly and stubborn. I'd thought that was the reason people liked her more. It had taken me a while to realize that the reason had nothing to do with who we were *inside*.

But maybe my father was right, and the two were closely connected. I'd always known people didn't like me as much as they liked my sister, and *that* was what had made me fierce. Maybe I would have been as sweet as Darina if I'd also walked through a world cushioned by everyone's approval of me.

Probably not, though.

"Honestly," I said, "you never paid that much attention to either of us. It was hard to tell the difference."

My father flinched. And where Darina, probably, would have felt guilty, I felt savagely glad. Now I *wanted* to hurt him, because he was hurting me.

"If you had paid attention," I added, "you'd know that I would *never* give up on Darina. No matter what."

"Really?" my father said. "Even if she goes ahead and marries the Beast?"

My jaw clenched so hard it hurt to speak. "Yes. Even then. I'll love her no matter what."

"I love her, too, Mera. But that doesn't stop me from seeing what's possible, and what's not possible."

"Because love is just an emotion," I said harshly, throwing his own words back at him. "It doesn't change who you truly are."

"Exactly."

Did he realize I was talking about him, and not about Darina? I couldn't tell. I supposed it didn't matter. "You don't *know* who Darina really is! I'm the one who knows her, and I'm telling you, I can get her to—"

"—agree with you?" he finished.

"That's not what this is about! I'm trying to save her."

"But you can't." He leaned forward. "You can only save yourself. Come with me, Mera."

I couldn't find a response. I opened my mouth, meaning to say something biting, and what came out was "Don't go."

He looked at me in complete silence.

"Please," I whispered.

He turned and walked to the door. He pulled down the handle and opened it.

He had left dozens of times before. If not for the past hour, it wouldn't even have hurt. So I told myself as I watched him shut the door behind him.

I stood without moving. I didn't realize that I was waiting for the door to open again until I heard, from the back of the house, the thud of the horse's hooves and the clatter of the cart.

I drew in a long, shaky breath, and on the exhale I shifted into a hound.

It was a sensible decision. I could travel through the woods faster that way. I could better discern what lurked among the trees, could better track which way Darina had gone, could better make my way through the castle.

It had nothing to do with the fact that hounds don't cry.

21

I was halfway to the castle when the howling began.

I had not been running for long—hounds travel faster than humans—and I skidded to a stop, my fur prickling all over. I pointed my muzzle at the sky. The howls filled the air, a series of high, throaty yips that crescendoed into an endless, ghostly cry.

When the hounds howled, they did so with a purpose: to call the pack to the Hunt, to warn of danger, to find each other. I knew what all those howls meant, but I didn't know what this one was for. It rose and fell, a long and haunting chorus, expressing nothing but . . .

. . . but grief.

I *did* know what it meant. But I didn't know why the pack was grieving.

I plunged into the stream, swimming briefly through

its deepest part, and raced up the other side of the ravine without even pausing to shake my fur dry.

By the time I reached the castle, the howling had gone silent. I didn't know if that was a good sign or a bad sign, but I did know it would make it easier to shift back into a girl, without that wild call shivering through my body. So I pushed myself into my other form, as fast as I could, using all my strength—

Which I didn't need. I was human within seconds, crouched on quivering arms and legs, my hair in bedraggled tangles over my eyes. It had been as easy as if I had never entered this castle, never run with the Hunt, never been subject to the Beast's command.

I also didn't know if *that* was a good or bad sign. But if I had to guess: *bad.*

I straightened, tried to brush my hair out of my face—it flopped right back in the same spot—and shoved at the castle door. It didn't budge. I threw myself against it, pushing with all my might, and finally it creaked slightly open. I squeezed through a gap that was barely big enough for me and stumbled into the pitch-black hall. Not a single candle was lit. I couldn't see my hands in front of my face.

"DARINA!" I screamed.

Something whispered past me in the shadows. I

recognized the light patter of paws on stone, the faint rustle of fur.

"Where is she?" I gasped. "Take me to her!"

The hound padded away from me. I thought of shifting again—as a hound, I could navigate with smell and sound even in the darkness—but I squashed the urge. Not here, not inside the castle.

I followed the hound as best I could, my footsteps echoing against the stone walls. Then it stopped and made a low sound, somewhere between a growl and a whimper. I stopped, too, and reached forward. My hand touched wood—so we had crossed the hall and reached a door. I slid my hand sideways, looking for a handle, and my fingers brushed against glass.

I snatched my hand back. Beside me, the hound yipped, and its cool nose prodded my calf insistently.

"What—" I whispered, and then I heard a muffled sob. Darina.

I put my hand flat on the glass and *pushed*. There was a moment of resistance, and then my hand went through the mirror. A thick, cool sensation surrounded my skin. I gritted my teeth and pushed harder.

Something grabbed my fingers, something long and thin and scaly, and a woman's high, mocking laugh rang through the room.

I screamed and pulled my hand back. The fingers let me go, and I fell backward onto the stone floor. Pain shot up my back, bringing tears to my eyes. I shoved my fists against my mouth, because if I started crying now, I wasn't sure when I would stop.

"That's not Darina," I said accusingly.

The hound's growl was, unmistakably, annoyed. I heard its paws thud against wood, and then the creak of a door handle.

"Oh!" I scrambled to my feet. "Through the *door*, not through the mirror?"

The hound snorted.

I reached for the door handle, yanked it down, and pushed the door open.

On the other side was the rose garden, flooded with moonlight. Darina knelt in the center of the path, sobbing. The garden was a mess: petals plucked and flung all over, stems trampled, the scent of crushed flowers thick in the air. Petals covered Darina's hair and dress, their brilliant colors bleached pale by the moonlight.

I stopped in the doorway, and the hound slipped past me. It went to Darina and licked her neck. It was a female hound with jet-black fur and a lean, graceful muzzle. She nudged Darina's cheek, then looked at me, her eyes liquid gold.

I stepped toward her and whispered, "Mother?"

I hadn't planned to say it. But as it turned out, that was the only word that could have caught Darina's attention just then. She looked up, her face wet with tears, and stared at the black hound.

A tingle ran through the air, and the hound shimmered and changed. I saw the green dress first, and then her face, surrounded by a waterfall of jet-black hair.

"*Ressa?*" I said.

Ressa didn't even look at me. She straightened and stared down at Darina, the hem of her dress swishing against the floor.

"You have to find him," she said. "Before it's too late."

My throat worked as I tried to form words. My mind had gone blank with shock. It was only when Darina let out a small, choked wail that I was able to say, "*How?*"

I wasn't even sure what I was asking. But Ressa answered anyway.

"I've been able to shift since I was your age," she said. "I didn't want to be stuck as a hound ... Talya needs me ... so I went to the Beast and struck a bargain. I told him it would be useful to have someone in the village who could help get goods to the castle and keep an ear out for any signs that the villagers might be massing against him." She met my eyes. "He warned me that he had made that bargain before, with your mother. It worked for a while; she switched back and forth, from human to

hound, avoiding making a final choice. Until one day . . .
she couldn't." She knelt, speaking to Darina instead of
to me. "The Beast told me your mother couldn't accept
being stuck in hound form while her husband and children were human. She stole a petal off the Beast's last
rose and ate it in an attempt to change back. But she
couldn't. She couldn't shift, and she wouldn't stop trying, until finally her heart gave out." She swallowed. "I
think . . . I think that's what's happening to the Beast
now."

"It's my fault," Darina whispered.

"No," Ressa said. "It's mine." She looked up at me, her
hair falling over her shoulders. "I heard you and your
father in the tavern. I thought you had convinced Darina
to leave with you, and I . . . I told the Beast. I told him so
he could *stop* it. I thought he would chase after you and
get her back. Instead, he . . . he . . ."

She shook her head.

"Instead he what?" I said harshly. The way they both
looked at me made me feel like *I* was the monster, but I
went on. "Sent you to stop us and drag her back?"

"No," Ressa said. She took Darina's hand. "He said that
if you wanted to go, he was going to let you."

"I didn't want to go," Darina choked. "You didn't hear
their whole conversation. I was—"

She looked at me, and I braced myself. The grief

on her face drained my anger and left me no defense against my guilt.

But there was no anger on *her* face. Something I didn't understand at all.

"It was just a mistake," she finished. "What did he do, Ressa?"

"He said he was going to change into a man," Ressa said. "He thought you were leaving because he was a Beast. And that if he changed, you might decide to come back."

"How?" I demanded. "I thought he couldn't find the rose on his own."

"He said he would go through every mirror in the castle if he had to." Ressa swallowed. "I don't think he actually believed it would work. But you know how this castle is. If you're desperate enough, it will take you where you need to go. I guess he was finally desperate enough."

"He didn't have to be." Darina shook her head frantically. "He didn't have to do this. I was already on my way back. I would never have left him."

"It's not too late," Ressa said urgently. "If he was dead, some of the hounds would have shifted back to human already. They're all still bound to be part of the pack, and that means he's alive."

Darina got to her feet. "I have to find him. I have to tell him that he doesn't have to—I have to make him *stop*. Where is he, Ressa?"

"I don't know," Ressa said.

They both turned and looked at me.

"How would *I* know?" I protested. But even as I said it, I realized that I did know.

Darina went perfectly still, and when she spoke, it was barely louder than a breath. "Mera. Please."

I looked back at her and saw her expression shift as she realized the truth. I was, *finally*, the one in control. Not locked in a cell, not forced into the shape of a hound, not cowering before the Beast's rage. Not blindsided by Darina's betrayal. Now *I* was the one who could make *her* do what she should have done all along.

"Don't," Darina said. "I know you're angry, Mera, but please don't do this to me."

Her voice broke, and the hurt in it was like a lance, draining my victory in one quick second. I saw again that small white note, the tear-smudged handwriting:

Please don't hate me.

I had been so angry. So sure Darina didn't care how I felt. I'd been determined that if she didn't care, neither would I.

But she did care. I had been hurting her, too.

"I don't know where he is," I said. "But I have a pretty good guess."

Darina smiled, even as tears continued to pour down her cheeks. "Thank you."

I couldn't say *You're welcome.* I couldn't say anything. It felt like something thick and foul-tasting had lodged in my throat.

So I turned and walked out of the garden, without looking back to confirm that anyone was following me.

Back in the great hall, the candles were now lit, filling the stone space with shifting, flickering shadows. The howling had resumed, rising and falling, an endless, unearthly lament. It made me shiver all over.

"*Hurry,*" Darina breathed.

I led them up the stairs, then turned and began to jog alongside the railing. The balcony seemed to stretch far longer than I remembered, door after identical door, each wall sconce holding exactly one lit candle.

A stitch began to burrow into my side, and I wondered if the door I was looking for was still there. What if it was just a stretch of wall now? Would Darina believe me when I said I couldn't find it?

And then there it was, the handle still tilted downward from when I had pulled it in blind desperation. The door had not latched shut, and I pushed it open with one hand.

I was in luck. Or maybe the castle wanted me to succeed. The door opened onto the same narrow, window-lined passageway I'd raced down just last night with a hound's saliva splattering on my heels.

I'd known, even then, that it didn't make sense for this passageway to lead nowhere.

It also didn't make sense that the windows of the passageway faced the outdoors—but they did, and moonlight streaked through them to form a zigzag pattern in the narrow hallway. Darina's face flickered in and out of the brightness as we ran toward the dead end, Ressa right behind us.

Glass crunched beneath our feet, and I spared a moment to wonder who had broken the original mirror that had once hung here. Probably the Beast himself, in one of his rages. Whatever he'd seen in the mirror must have been terrible.

There was a new mirror at the end of the hall now, suspended by the nails I had once desperately hoped would open a doorway.

Which they did. Once you hung a mirror on them.

In the mirror's reflection, I saw my sister's mouth form a grim line. I saw her straighten.

"Darina!" I grabbed her skirt. "Wait—"

She rushed forward. The fabric was ripped from my hand, and my sister plunged straight through the mirror and vanished.

22

I went right after her, of course.

It felt like plunging into thick, ice-cold water—including the inability to breathe. I opened my mouth, gasping, and nothing rushed in. But it only lasted a second, and then I was stumbling onto a stone floor, gulping in cool, stale-smelling air.

I leapt to my feet. I was in a large, round room made completely of stone. There were no decorations of any kind—no rugs, no tapestries—but the stone itself was made of different colors and shapes, fitted together in a pattern that I could almost, but not quite, make out. There were no windows, but some of the stones seemed to be glowing, and they filled the room with a dim light that didn't touch the shadows.

There was only one piece of furniture in the room: a round wooden table, atop which sat the crystal vase I had seen before in a mirror. But this time, the rose drooping from the vase did not have even a single petal clinging to it. There was just that thorny little stump, its emptiness like a wound.

Darina let out a cry. She rushed past the table and threw herself to her knees, and I saw that one of the shadows on the floor was the still, sprawled form of a monster, half-covered by a length of ratty blanket, its legs stretched stiff and its clawed fingers spread out helplessly.

"Beast!" Darina cried. "No! Please, no!"

I became aware again of the howling, which had never stopped. It rose and fell in a tuneless pattern, high and hollow and aching.

"Beast," Darina said, her voice shaking. "Beast, I love you. Please don't die."

The giant mass of fur and sinew didn't budge. He might not be dead yet, but it was a matter of minutes. Soon the howling would stop, and then—if Ressa was right—the forest would be full of humans. Of the people the Beast had taken from us, coming back home.

Darina would come home, too. She would grieve, and eventually she would recover. She would marry Sederic, or she would leave the village someday and sail away to find our father, or she would do something else entirely. She could do whatever she wanted. Someday she would look back and be glad she hadn't bound her life to a beast.

Someday she would realize that I had been right.

"Beast," Darina said. Or tried to say. Her voice broke.

I looked again at the bare, ragged flower stem. The reason the Beast had gone after my family in the first place, had kept Darina and then me prisoner.

But he hadn't gone after her when he thought she was escaping. Instead, he had eaten the last petal himself.

So that she could have a choice.

Darina was weeping silently now. Her tears fell on the Beast's fur, and her shoulders shook.

She wasn't looking at me. Not this time. She didn't think there was anything I could do. If I kept silent, she would never know.

I crossed the room in two quick steps and knelt beside my sister. I pulled my pouch out from under the neck of my dress.

"Here," I said. "Try this."

Darina looked up, her face streaked with tears. Her eyes were swollen and red, her face ravaged with uneven creases. It was only then that I realized I was crying, too.

I yanked the pouch free. Which didn't work; Grandma's threads were woven thick and tough. I tried twice, then gave up and pulled the loop over my head.

"Open his mouth," I said.

Without hesitation, Darina grabbed the Beast's jaws

and pulled them open. His teeth were long and curved, and his tongue flopped sideways. I pulled the pouch open and spilled every last bit of my powder toward the back of the Beast's throat.

Darina forced his jaws shut.

For a long moment nothing happened. Then the Beast's jaw spasmed and his throat worked. He made a low, groaning sound that was both inhuman and un-wolflike.

His eyes opened wide. His back arched, and he howled.

"Beast!" Darina screamed, and I grabbed her arm and pulled her off him. To my surprise, she didn't fight me. She knew it was dangerous to be near an animal in pain, no matter how tame it was.

The Beast's paws scrabbled at the air, and his head went back.

It was the howl that changed first, morphing slowly from a savage, animal sound to a human shriek. The rest of him followed. His fur shrank into his skin, his body lengthened and straightened, his face flattened and re-formed.

And he screamed the whole time.

When it ended, I knew by the silence. And by Darina wrenching free of me and stumbling to her knees next to the human man lying on the floor.

"Beast?" she said.

He turned his head. His eyes were still amber, but they no longer glowed. He had a lean, angular face, with a bony nose and a long jaw.

"Darina?" His voice was hoarse and scratchy, like a machine that needed oiling. He lifted himself up on one arm, pulling the blanket with him. "Is it . . . are you really here?"

Needless to say, they fell into each other's arms.

I got to my feet, trying to find somewhere else to look. The stone patterns, it turned out, made me dizzy if I stared at them too long. My pouch was on the floor, and Darina's foot was on it. I didn't have much hope of getting her attention, so I pushed her foot out of the way. She didn't notice.

There was still a bit of powder clinging to the bottom of the pouch. I tied the pouch up, put it over my head, and tucked it under my shirt.

By then, Darina and the Beast had finally finished kissing. They got to their feet, holding hands. The Beast used his other hand to hold the blanket wrapped around his body. It dangled halfway to his knees and looked ridiculous.

"Mera." Darina let go of the Beast's hand and walked over to me. "Thank you."

I kept my focus on my sister's familiar face, on her

wide, beaming smile and shining eyes. Her gaze met mine, and I looked down.

She had been right all along, and I had been wrong. He *did* love her.

But love was just a feeling, and feelings could go away.

"I still don't think you should marry him," I said.

Darina lifted her eyebrows. "Really, Mera? You should have said something."

I laughed, surprising myself. "I also think," I said, "that we need to get out of here."

Darina looked around the room, and seemed to notice for the first time that there was no door. Her eyes widened.

"It's all right," the Beast told her. His voice was gentle—*actually* gentle, which, I realized, he had never quite managed before. "I've been in this room before. We're in the basement."

"I thought the castle didn't have a basement," I said.

"It doesn't," the Beast replied.

"Well, that's reassuring." I stepped farther away from him and turned in a slow circle, examining the walls. "How do we get *out* of this nonexistent basement?"

He smiled at me. I did not smile back. He removed his hand from Darina's, walked over to the wall, and splayed his fingers carefully across various stones.

A section of the wall swung outward to reveal a winding stairway going up.

I tried to exchange a glance with Darina. But she had already rushed forward to take the Beast's hand again. (Did he have a name now, other than "the Beast"? If he did, I supposed I would have to use it eventually.) They started up the stairs together, and I trailed behind them.

The stairs opened into the entrance hall. As we emerged onto the stone floor, the front door opened, letting in a flood of morning sunlight and a mass of people and hounds.

The hounds bounded over to the Beast, tails lashing back and forth. The people all dropped into curtsies and bows.

"My lord," one of them said, rising. He was a man in a weirdly shaped velvet outfit that looked like it belonged in an old portrait. His eyes were the exact same moss green as Sederic's. He bowed again to the Beast, and then to Darina.

"My lady," he said. "Your love and gentleness has freed us. Our gratitude is as endless as the sea, and our admiration as powerful as its waves."

Yup. Definitely one of Sederic's ancestors.

More people rose and came toward us, dressed in an array of widely varying fashions. The Beast strode forward to meet them, looking as noble as he possibly could while clutching a blanket around his waist. For just a moment, nobody was paying attention to me and Darina. I looked up at her, trying to decide how best to get her attention. But she was already looking down at me. She leaned forward and grabbed my hands. Her eyes shone.

"You will come to the wedding," she said. "Won't you?"

I just looked at her, and her smile faded, the joy in her eyes dimming.

My father had been wrong about so much, but he had been right about one thing. I didn't just want to stop this marriage. I wanted Darina to *agree* with me. I wanted my sister back, for things between us to be the way they had been before.

And I would never have that.

But whatever we could have, it would be better than the burning bitterness I was still carrying inside me. I didn't know how to let it go, so I pushed it aside.

"Yes," I said. "Of course I'll come to your wedding."

Her face lit up. She hugged me, and I hugged her back tightly.

"I'll be your bridesmaid," Ressa said from behind me. I whirled; I hadn't noticed her coming down the stairs. "I'll need a new dress. I'm sure the Beast can pay for that, right? Maybe a yellow theme—and Mera, of course, will be the flower girl—"

I winced, glancing at the door that led to the rose garden.

"Tulips," Darina said firmly. "You'll carry tulips."

"Fine," I said. "But I'm not wearing yellow."

She pursed her lips. "I really think—"

"Darina," the Beast called, and she broke off immediately. He reached out a hand to her, and she stepped toward him, giving me one quick glance over her shoulder.

"We'll talk about your dress later," she said.

"No," I said. "We won't."

I couldn't tell if she heard me. People were grabbing her hands, and hounds were jumping up to lick her face, and the Beast/man with the blanket around his stomach was beaming down at her. The noise was overwhelming.

Maybe not just the noise.

It was too crowded to make it through as a girl, but it turned out I could still shift into a hound. My fur was tingling with the speed of my shift as I squeezed between legs and under hands.

Something yipped, and I paused as Leo bounded through the door, ears pricked forward. He sniffed me, and I sniffed back. I could smell his curiosity and eagerness. Everything was different now, and he found it exciting.

I padded across the marble floor of the entrance hall and squeezed through the still-open door. Then I raced through the woods toward home, leaving the castle and the crowd—and my sister—temporarily behind.

⇒ EPILOGUE ⇐

The wedding was beautiful. Even I had to admit it.

They held it outdoors, in a large field behind the castle walls. It was two months after the Beast had turned human—Grandma had insisted that she needed the time to get ready—and it was a cold but beautiful night, the branches glittering with ice, the guests' breath frosting the air. Darina wore a dress draped with lace and embroidered with pearls. Her hair was arranged in an intricate design of tiny braids, which Ressa had worked on for three solid hours. Her face was radiant, her skin and eyes glowed.

The Beast was dressed in purple, with a gold-laced black cape that wrapped around his shoulders. His smile, as wide as Darina's, revealed slightly crooked teeth. His eyes were still amber, which made him look not-quite-human despite his new form.

"He *is* handsome," Ressa said rapturously, which was

blatantly not true. But that cape *did* look expensive enough to buy a whole village with, so I guessed that counted toward his looks.

He had a human name now. But in my mind, I still called him the Beast. Someone had to remember what he truly was.

Darina called him Beast, too, but she did it *fondly*. I did my best not to let her know what I thought about that.

I had borrowed an old blue frock of Talya's that Madam Nikkia had altered to my measurements. It didn't fit perfectly, but it didn't much matter. No one was looking at me.

Darina walked down the aisle herself. She hadn't asked me or Grandma to walk her down, which I was both grateful for and irritated by. It was only when I watched her walk toward the Beast alone that I realized the reason: she had been hoping until the very last minute that our father would do it.

My grandmother *had* given me a wedding invitation for my father, addressed to his secretary in one of the largest ports. She had told me to bring it to the inn and ask Ressa to give it to the next traveler headed for a ship. I had considered crumpling it up and throwing it away. In the end, I had simply done what Grandma asked. I didn't think it would make a difference.

And I had been right. There was still no sign of him.

Grandma and Darina sometimes talked as if he might show up someday, but I was sure he never would.

When the Beast slid the ring onto Darina's finger—the white-gold ring with its flower-shaped quartz stone—Talya and Ressa both sobbed so loudly they had to be escorted into the woods to get themselves under control. Sederic did the escorting. Despite his stoic heartbreak, he was extremely solicitous of Ressa.

After the ceremony, the Beast made a lengthy speech describing the events that had led to this "unbelievably joyous and beautiful day," using language that made Sederic's wedding song seem understated by comparison. He skimmed rather quickly over the whole kidnapping issue, left *me* out of the story entirely, and ended by drawing Darina to her feet and gazing deeply into her eyes.

"For so many years," he said, "I thought I couldn't turn back into a man. But the truth was that I didn't want to badly enough." He smiled down at her. "The cure wasn't in the roses after all. It was in finding someone who made me *want* to be a man."

I snorted. I mean, let's be honest. The cure kind of *was* in the roses.

Luckily, no one heard me over the cheers.

When Darina and I danced together, it felt for a short stretch of time like it was just the two of us again. As if after the wedding, we'd be going home together to sleep in the same room.

Darina smiled at me, radiantly happy, and in that moment, I didn't think about the past or the future. I was just happy that she was happy.

Then she whirled away to dance with the rest of her guests. Some were people I had never seen until a few months ago, men and women in old-fashioned clothes who had broken free of their hound forms when the Beast did. But there were also hounds on the flattened grass, circling the tables and snatching unattended leftovers, occasionally dashing among the dancers and causing chaos. Some of the pack had decided not to try to turn back. Or had decided not to try *yet*.

Or maybe some of them had always been hounds. Like Leo, who was trying to get at the slices of wedding cake stacked on a long wooden table. He couldn't quite reach the table, so he kept jumping straight up, his paws barely brushing the wooden edge. Every time, he fell straight back down, then sprang up again. He did it over and over with barely a pause between failures, until finally he managed to get hold of the tabletop with his front paws and hold on, hind legs scrabbling furiously against the table leg. Just as I started forward to help him, he managed to hoist himself up high enough to grab the edge of the cake tray in his jaws.

He went over backward, and the tray went with him. He landed on his back, paws flailing in the air, then righted himself with a twist and pounced delightedly on the cake now smashed all over the grass.

I made my way to the edge of the dancers, where Grandma was seated on a plush chair, her legs covered by her favorite blue blanket. Her eyes were closed, and the faint beginnings of a snore became audible as I reached her.

"Are you tired?" I asked. "I can take you home."

Grandma's eyes popped open. "I'm not tired."

"Is that because I just woke you up?"

"Don't be impertinent." She struggled upright and looked around. "I want a piece of cake."

"I'm not sure that's possible."

A howl, sudden and throaty, rose from the hounds at the feast. Leo gobbled down the last bit of cake, lifted his head, and joined in with a series of joyful yips. Then he dashed away from the table and barreled across the grass, leaving paw prints in the frosting as he raced to join the hounds streaming into the woods.

The Beast watched them go, his face tight. Over the past two months, he hadn't shifted into his hound form once. I had thought it was just because he was on his best behavior. But now it occurred to me that maybe he was afraid to. Afraid he wouldn't be able to shift back.

He had still found a way to hunt, though.

He whistled, and a tall, dappled horse trotted obediently onto the field, shaking its mane. The Beast had bought the horse from a trader two months ago, for an amount of money that had made Ressa upgrade him to "*extraordinarily* handsome." (The Beast, not the horse.)

Now the Beast crossed the lawn in several long strides and swung himself onto the horse's back. He reached down for Darina.

She grabbed his hand, leapt as he pulled, and landed gracefully in front of him. She sat sideways, her gown trailing dramatically down the horse's side (which, I could tell, irritated the horse), and smiled up at him. Then she looked over the Beast's shoulder at me.

I crossed my arms over my chest. My fingers curved into my sleeve like claws, and I felt sharpness prick through the delicate fabric.

The Beast spurred his steed, and they were gone. From deep within the trees, the hounds howled, calling the pack together for the Hunt.

"Why don't you go with them?" Grandma asked.

I *wanted* to go with them. My skin itched from the inside. I imagined running with the pack, answering those howls, joining with them in a wild and vicious and glorious Hunt.

But I wouldn't. I wouldn't be what the Beast had told

me I was. I, too, had not shifted into hound form a single time since my flight from the castle two months ago. It felt like my last protest, my one remaining way to show that all was not forgotten.

I raised my eyebrows at Grandma. "What, so you're okay with my shifting now?"

I sounded childish and sullen. But Grandma didn't rebuke me. She shrugged and said, in an unruffled voice, "Of course. I was only against it because it was dangerous. It isn't dangerous anymore."

"Isn't it? I could still get stuck in the form of a hound."

"Unlikely," she said. "Now that the Beast is a man, the pull of the pack isn't what it was."

"Assuming he decides to stay a man."

Grandma tilted her head to look at me, her wispy eyebrows rising. I braced myself for a rebuke.

But all she said was, "If you're right about him, Darina's going to need you someday."

After a long silence, I said, "I know."

"Then you should make sure," Grandma said, "that you'll be there for her when she does."

My stomach roiled. At first I thought it was anger, but when I pushed the anger away, other feelings bubbled up. I took a deep breath and admitted, "I'm afraid."

"You won't have any trouble shifting back," she said.

"But what if I don't want to shift back?" I looked at the

woods so I wasn't meeting her eyes. "What if I want to be a hound more than I want to be a girl? Or what if I don't know what I want, and I make the wrong decision, and then I'm stuck with it?"

"You have plenty of time to worry about that." Grandma stretched her neck from side to side. I heard something crack, and it sounded painful, but she smiled with evident relief. "Tonight we have a simpler decision to make."

The blanket fell off her lap. Her fingers were short and sharp, lined with white fur.

My shock drove all my roiling, conflicting feelings right out of my body. "You can shift?"

"Where did you think you inherited it from?"

"But . . ." I felt suddenly foolish. "We never saw you!"

"Of course you didn't. I made sure of that."

"So you—" I didn't even know where to start with questions. "All this time you—you decided to live your whole life as a human?"

"I did no such thing." She rolled her eyes, which were now distinctly yellow. "I haven't exactly lived my *whole* life yet."

I stared at her.

"Pups." She shook her head. "So dramatic. Always thinking you have to make every big decision when you're young." She got to her feet. "I'm still thinking it over."

And then she was on four legs, not two. She was pure white, her fur slightly wispy, her body bonier than a younger hound's would have been. But her eyes were clear and her movements agile.

She barked at me sharply, and I understood what she wanted.

We left the tables and the human dancers behind. We caught up to Darina first; she blinked down at us from horseback, with just a hint of surprise, and I yelped at her. She grinned down at me.

Then Grandma and I raced ahead of the Beast and took the lead. The moonlight gleamed on our fur, our breath frosty in the chill night air, and Darina's delighted laugh floated behind us as we raced side by side through the night to join the pack for the evening's Hunt.

Acknowledgments

Some books are harder to write than others, and this book was definitely one of them. I could not have managed it without the guidance of my editors at Delacorte Press. Wendy Loggia and Ali Romig, thank you so much for your insightful edits and guidance. Thank you especially for telling me I had to take that original manuscript apart and then put it back together. It is now the book it was meant to be.

Thank you to all the fantastic people at Delacorte Press and Random House Children's Book, especially Brennan Bond, Hope Breeman, Colleen Fellingham, Alison Kolani, Tamar Schwartz, and Megan Shortt. Thank you to Michelle Cunningham and Maxine Vee for yet another amazing cover. Thank you to my wonderful agent, Andrea Somberg.

As always, I leaned heavily on the insights of my invaluable critique partners. Thank you so much to my early readers (some of whom also became this-revision-is-due-in-one-week readers!): Christine Amsden, Sima

Braunstein, Eliezer Gorfajn, Seth Z. Herman, Shlomo Sheril, and Tova Suslovich.

Thank you to Hadassah Cypess, who heard the earliest version of all and then the latest (there are both pitfalls and advantages to having a mother who is an author!), and to Shoshana Cypess, who waited very patiently while I revised and revised, and then was extremely helpful when I read her the almost-final version.

And last but definitely not least, thank you to Diana Peterfreund for letting me talk at you about this book for hours. On to the next one!

Meet the Pied Piper's little sister,
Clare, who is determined to uncover
the truth behind her brother's
seemingly cruel actions. . . .

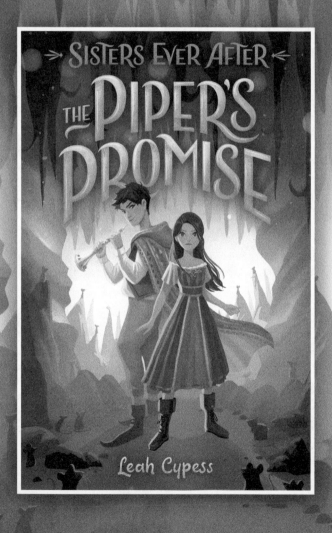

SISTERS EVER AFTER

THE PIPER'S PROMISE

Leah Cypess

1

The parents were grieving, and their grief was terrible to bear. Both because of the depth and sharpness of their sadness, and because I knew that if anything horrible ever happened to me or Tom, our mother would never grieve for us that way.

I wasn't sure she would grieve for us at all.

Love is a burden, Tom told me once, that time when I almost got eaten by a sea serpent and our mother laughed as she told the fae court about it. Tom had been the one to save me, and then to hold me tight as I coughed up water. But when I came to him sobbing over our mother's lack of caring, he had pressed his lips together impatiently. *The other side of love is pain.*

I saw that pain now as I walked through the shabby gray streets of Hamelin. It leaked from every window in this small, dusty town, glared from every tear-streaked face that watched me pass.

I understood that grief. For weeks now, I had been missing my brother—a constant, empty ache under my heart. I knew how powerful that anguish was, because it had led me to do the unthinkable: to leave the Realms, by myself, and come to the human world to find him.

And I would find him. I *would*. No matter what had happened to him, no matter what he had done, I would find him and we would be together again.

But I had never imagined that I was going to find *this*. Not my brother, but the pain he had left behind. And the only thing that made it bearable was the determination I clung to: *I can fix this*.

I didn't know for sure if that was true. But I forced myself to believe it, because there was no other way I could have made it down that eerily silent street, up the stairs of the grandest house in town, and into the mayor's office.

The mayor's "office" was actually the front room of his house, which says a lot about how often Hamelin's yearly elections resulted in a change of mayor. Mayor Herman, I'd been told, had been the mayor for over twenty years. It would probably help if someone occasionally ran *against* him, but since no one ever did, the ballots generally had two choices: *Herman Jeremson* and *Somebody Else, If We Can Find Someone Qualified and Willing,*

Which Is Unlikely. Written on the ballot, just like that—I'd seen one stuck under a grimy well stone, left over from the last election.

Not the most democratic of places, Hamelin. Not that it would have helped much if it had been.

The mayor's office reeked of stale tobacco, and his face shone with sweat. He sat upright in his brown leather chair, brow furrowed, as if he was in control of the situation. But I, of all people, could recognize tightly controlled fear. *He* had been the one who hired my brother as a ratcatcher. *He* had been the one who refused to pay the exorbitant fee. Any moment now, the people's grief would turn into anger, and they would remember who was responsible for the tragedy that had overtaken their town.

They would be wrong. My brother had come for their children, and he would have found a way to take them even if Hamelin had a smart and honest mayor.

But nobody knew that except me. And I certainly wasn't about to tell Mayor Herman.

The mayor looked up as I entered. He drew in his breath, and I wondered if he recognized something in me that reminded him of Tom. If he was remembering the last time a lanky, dark-haired child had walked into his office and offered to solve his problems.

I hoped not. But I had to be careful, just in case.

"Mayor Herman," I said, and curtsied. His eyes widened in astonishment, from which I gathered that it was not customary to curtsy to mayors. Human etiquette rules were so confusing. "I am here to help you get Hamelin's children back."

"Are you?" He sat back, regarding me with sharp blue eyes. "And what payment will you ask in return?"

I had expected either joy or disbelief. I knew then that something was wrong, but I couldn't think fast enough to change my plan. "No payment. I only want to make sure the children are unharmed. Can you tell me which way they went?"

The mayor leaned forward as if listening. But his eyes flicked to the door behind me.

Too late, I realized what was happening.

I turned, but not fast enough. Two men burst into the room. One had a bristling black beard that stuck straight out from his chin, the other a large, furry mustache that looked like it had been glued crookedly to his face. Before I could move, the man with the mustache had my arms pinned behind my back. I tried to twist free, but the bearded man grabbed my right arm and snapped a thick iron band around my wrist.

After that, the only thing I could do was scream.

I did scream, at the top of my lungs. Of course, no

one came to help me. The townspeople were not partial to mysterious strangers right now.

The bearded man stepped away from me. "Should I slap her," he asked, "to shut her up?"

He sounded like he really wanted to. I gulped, silencing myself.

"Good girl," the mayor said. He came out from behind his desk and stood in front of me. The mustached man still had my arms pinned behind me and the bearded one glowered at me from beside the mayor. Each was nearly twice my height, but the mayor still made sure to leave several yards between him and me.

It was nice to have a reputation.

It would have been even nicer if I deserved that reputation.

I snarled at the mayor. He flinched, then puffed his chest out. Too late; I had seen the flinch, and so had his hairy-faced henchmen.

"You *will* get us our children back," he said. "And I'll give you nothing in return except your worthless life."

From the way the bearded man looked at him sideways, I knew the mayor had no intention of giving me that, either.

"Tell us where they are," the mayor said.

"I don't know!" I gasped. The iron band on my wrist hurt—not as much as it would have if I was fully fae, but still, it felt like hives were breaking out wherever it touched my skin. "I swear, I don't know! That's why I came here, so you could tell me which way they went."

The bearded man strode forward and struck me in the face, so hard my head snapped to one side.

The mayor opened his mouth as if to object, then closed it. He looked very proper in his fine dark clothes, his trim beard a distinguished blend of gray and white. But when the man raised his hand again, Mayor Herman didn't tell him to stop.

"Where did you take them?" he demanded.

"I didn't take them anywhere! Do I *look* like the Pied Piper to you?"

Which was a foolish question. Of course I did.

I had made a mistake, coming here. I had thought I understood humans better than I did. Tom had warned me about exactly that—*Just because we were born human, doesn't mean we know how to think like them. We've lived our whole lives among the fae.* I should have paid more attention.

To the fae, Tom and I were nearly identical. They got us mixed up constantly. But humans could tell us apart easily—even Anna, who had trouble telling most people apart. I had once asked her how she did it, and she had burst into laughter and said, "Are you joking? He's several handsbreadth taller than you!"

But apparently, even to humans, Tom and I looked similar. We *were* brother and sister. Thin, dark-haired, and dark-eyed, with bony jaws and jutting cheekbones.

"I'm not the piper!" I shouted. "I'm not the one who stole your children!"

"Give us a straight answer," the man behind me growled.

The mayor motioned him into silence. "Where did you and your brother take our children?"

"I didn't," I said. "It was just him." After a too-long pause, I added, "I'm sorry."

"I've heard," the mayor said, "that the fae can't lie. But if you're human, then you'd be perfectly capable of lying, wouldn't you?"

The fae work very hard at spreading that rumor. They're actually quite good at lying. And I, personally, am *very* good at lying.

But as it happened, I was telling the truth. How to convince the mayor of that, though?

"My brother and I have spent most of our lives in the Faerie Realms," I said. "The magic of their land has seeped into us—through our skin, our breath, our food. It has made us somewhat fae, even though we were born fully human."

"What does that mean?"

"It means," I said, "that I can lie, but it would cause me great pain. I don't lie unless I have a good reason to. And I'm not lying now."

Mayor Herman clasped his hands behind his back and stepped forward diagonally—giving the impression that he was approaching me, while in reality keeping the same distance between us. "Say I believe you. Why did your brother take them?"

"I don't know why he took them." My skin had adjusted somewhat to the iron band, so the pain had become a dull, constant itch. It was still distracting, but not quite as much as having my arms held behind my back. "I haven't seen him in months."

"Are the children—" His voice caught. "Are they alive?"

I didn't know the answer to that. I didn't want to think Tom would actually let innocent children die. Then again, I was having trouble thinking about what he was doing. My mind kept shuddering back from it, as if ignoring it might make it not true.

I gave the mayor an answer anyhow. "They're alive. I'm sure he hasn't hurt them."

The mayor gave me an incredulous look. From his perspective, I suppose, Tom had already hurt them.

"If you don't know why he took them," the mayor said, "and you don't know where they are, how are you planning to get them back?"

"If that's really what you're planning," the bearded man added. This time, he ignored the mayor's silencing gesture. He was, I could tell, going to hit me again soon, whether the mayor liked it or not.

"I'll follow him," I said. "I can go wherever he can. If you show me which way he took the children, I'll track him down."

"And when you *do* catch up to your brother," the man with the mustache cut in, tightening his grip on my arms, "how do you plan to get the children away from him?"

"I know which spell he used," I said. "All I need to do is find him and I can break it."

Like I said: I'm *very* good at lying.

The truth was, the main thing I wanted from Tom was answers. He probably had a good reason for what he had done; for all I knew, he was saving the children, not stealing them. Once he explained everything to me, I might even end up helping him.

The mayor definitely didn't need to know that. So I said nothing else until he nodded abruptly and gestured at the man with the mustache.

My wrists were released so suddenly that I stumbled forward. I managed not to fall or to whimper from the pain in my shoulders. I straightened.

"Tell me which way he went," I said.

The mayor pressed his lips together. I could see that he still didn't trust me; he wasn't quite as foolish as I had assumed. Which shouldn't have surprised me. After all, if the mayor was really such a fool, how had he managed to stay mayor for almost twenty years now?

I knew what Tom would have said to that: *Because humans are fools, too.* Tom had a habit of forgetting that we were also human.

In the end, though, it didn't matter how smart the mayor was. I was the only person offering him a solution to his terrible situation. What could he do but take it?

Which was probably exactly what he had thought when Tom came to him the first time.

"When you come back with them," he said, "we'll pay you what we owe your brother."

"Sure," I agreed. Why not?

"And we'll take off the iron band."

From the way the mayor smiled, I knew my reaction had been visible. I forced my voice to stay even. "You need to take it off *now*. I can't work magic with iron on me. I won't be able to break the spell."

"That's why I'll come with you." He held up one hand. A tiny key dangled from it, swinging lightly back and forth. "When we catch up to the children, I'll take the band off."

If I showed panic, I was done. I forced myself steady, a maneuver that was very familiar to me. The fae liked to play with human children—to taunt and tease and frighten us—and their carelessness often led to human deaths. But if you showed no reaction, if you were a boring plaything, they would usually leave you alone.

So I had become very good at hiding fear. But usually Tom was right beside me, pretending along with me. He was the one who had taught me how to do it. I had never realized how much of my technique was actually just copying him.

I thought of how he would act now: calm, sure, rakish. I put a bit of his cockiness into my voice. "It's an excellent idea. But it won't work. No adult human can pass into the Faerie Realms. I couldn't take you with me even if I wanted to."

The mayor stepped back, looking lost. The bearded man stepped forward, hand swinging forward.

"Then take me," a voice said from the doorway.

About the Author

Leah Cypess is the author of *Thornwood, Glass Slippers,* and *The Piper's Promise,* the first three books in the Sisters Ever After series. She lives in the kingdom of Silver Spring, Maryland, with her family and wrote large parts of this book in a rose garden.

leahcypess.com